PRAISE FOR THE MADISON NIGHT MYSTERY SERIES

"A terrific mystery is always in fashion—and this one is sleek, chic and constantly surprising. Vallere's smart styling and wry humor combine for a fresh and original page-turner—it'll have you eagerly awaiting her next appealing adventure. I'm a fan!"

— Hank Phillippi Ryan,
Agatha, Anthony, Macavity and Mary Higgins Clark Award-Winning Author of *The Other Woman*

"All of us who fell in love with Madison Night in *Pillow Stalk* will be rooting for her when the past comes back to haunt her in *That Touch of Ink*. The suspense is intense, the plot is hot and the style is to die for. A thoroughly entertaining entry in this enjoyable series."

— Catriona McPherson,

decorating and fashion tips...Her disarmingly honest lead and two hunky sidekicks will appeal to all fashionistas and antiques types and have romance crossover appeal."

— *Library Journal*

"A multifaceted story...plenty of surprises...And what an ending!"

— Mary Marks,
New York Journal of Books

"If you are looking for an unconventional mystery with a snarky, no-nonsense main character, this is it...Instead of clashing, humor and danger meld perfectly, and there's a cliffhanger that will make your jaw drop."

— Abigail Ortlieb,
RT Book Reviews

"A charming modern tribute to Doris Day movies and the retro era of the '50s, including murders, escalating danger, romance...and a puppy!"

— Linda O. Johnston,
Author of the Pet Rescue Mysteries

"I love mysteries where I can't figure out who the real killer is until the end, and this was one of those. The novel was well written, moved at a smooth pace, and Madison's character was a riot."

"Strong mysteries, an excellent cast, chills, thrills and laughter, and an adorable dog... if you haven't read a Madison Night mystery, what are you waiting for?"

"The writing was crisp with a solid plot that kept me engaged with Madison, Tex and the other supporting cast."

"The strength of this series that Madison has changed, adapted, and grown over the course of the six books."

"...a well plotted mystery filled with great characters that will keep you hooked until you get to the final page."

"If you are looking for a suspenseful "whodunit" without the gore or horror of other genres, this book is definitely for you."

PLEASE DON'T

PUSH UP

THE DAISIES

A Madison Night Mystery

PLEASE DON'T PUSH UP THE DAISIES

A Madison Night Mystery #11

A Polyester Press Mystery

Polyester Press

www.polyesterpress.com

eBook ISBN: 9781954579743

Paperback ISBN: 9781954579750

Hardcover ISBN: 9781954579767

PLEASE DON'T PUSH UP THE DAISIES

A Madison Night Mystery

Diane Vallere

Polyester Press

CHAPTER ONE

"THIS IS THE LAST OF IT," TEX SAID FROM BEHIND THE WHEEL of a moving truck. A week of packing had left him looking a little worse for wear. He'd had help in the form of his sister's four boys, who ranged in age from ten to seventeen. They'd packed their belongings and their mother's. They were all moving from Austin to Dallas to be closer to Uncle Tex. I'd met Tex four years ago, and this would be the first time I saw him interact with them. I wasn't sure what to expect.

The passenger-side door opened and shut. Moments later, a boy, about ten years old, came around the front of the truck. He wore a catcher's mitt on his left hand and held a worn baseball in the other. His dark blond hair was sun bleached by his hairline. He had freckles on his nose, and one of his eyes squeezed shut as he stared up at me. "Are you Madison?" he asked pointedly.

"I am." I glanced at Tex, who flashed his lazy, sexy grin. I turned back to the boy. "Are you Adam?"

"Yeah." He socked the baseball into the mitt, freeing up his right hand.

"What position do you play?" I asked.

"Third base."

Behind me, more truck doors opened and slammed shut. Tex joined us. A few moments later, another boy, slightly older than Adam, joined him.

Tex took the mitt and ball from Adam, who lost a little of his ten-year-old bravado.

"Watch this," Tex told the boys. He handed me the ball and then backed away. After he put a suitable amount of distance between us, he nodded.

I pitched a line drive.

Tex caught it easily, but the resulting *thwump* when the ball hit the glove said everything the boys needed to know about my abilities with a baseball.

"You don't look like you can throw," Adam said. "Can you do other stuff?"

I glanced up at Tex. He raised his eyebrows suggestively. I bit back a smile and a retort intended for him and not a ten-year-old. "What kind of stuff do you like to do?"

"Catch frogs. Sometimes salamanders. I had a pet milk snake until he got out of the terrarium. My mom freaked. She's a sissy."

"Watch it," Tex said. "That's my sister you're talking about."

Adam made a face at Tex, who kept his expression tough. Clearly wanting Tex's approval, Adam apologized and then hung his head. Tex handed him the baseball that he'd caught from my pitch, and Adam ground it into the center of his catcher's mitt and sulked.

Tex's townhouse was the end unit in a development. His building housed eight units, three stories tall with rooftop patios overlooking the Dallas skyline. The units had a narrow paved path that ran the length of the building and an alley with a garage in the back. Tex's unit, being on the end, had an additional alley alongside of his, but today, we stood on the sidewalk next to the truck.

It was late afternoon, and the sunlight, mostly blocked by neighboring clusters of residences like Tex's, peeked over rooftops, casting distorted shadows over us. It was April, a few weeks past my birthday, which had mostly come and gone thanks to my request that no fuss be made. I shared a birthday with actress Doris Day, and birthday celebrations used to come in the form of movie parties with my family. When they were killed in a car accident thirty years ago, I kept the Doris Day elements as reminders of those days but downplayed the annual marking of time.

Tex turned to the other boy. "You and Adam can play catch, but I don't want to hear any windows getting broken. Understood?"

"Sure, Uncle Tex," the boy said. He and Adam headed toward the alley that ran behind Tex's house.

"Which one is that?" I asked.

"Gabe."

"How many more are there?"

"Two."

"Are you sure you can handle four boys on your own?"

Tex grinned again. "Boys are easy. I'll throw a couple of burgers on the grill and put on the Rangers game. If that doesn't entertain them, the strippers will."

"I hope Lily knows what kind of influence you'll be on her sons."

"Lily is grateful I offered to take them off her hands for the night. Who knows the last time she had time alone with another adult her age." He studied me. "What do you have planned?"

"Pretty much the same as you."

"Including the strippers?"

"Yes, but mine strip paint."

Tex laughed out loud. "Considering Lily's about to move into her ex-husband's house, she'll probably appreciate that more."

A Jeep pulled up behind the truck. The Jeep's driver was a teenage version of the two boys I'd already met, and the passenger was somewhere between them all in age. The driver had the window down and his arm propped on the door. The sun glinted off the face of his black rubber sports watch. "Hey, Tex!" he called. "Where should I park?"

"Around back," Tex said. "Last garage of the building. The remote's on your visor."

The teen nodded and backed the Jeep up.

"No 'Uncle Tex' from him?" I asked.

"That's David," Tex said. "He's seventeen. He sees me as his equal."

"Right, because seventeen and fifty-two are the same."

"Age is a state of mind."

"Then I'd say you have more in common with the thirteen-year-old."

"Gabe's twelve."

God help me.

Tex dropped the truck keys into my open hand. "The

address is in the GPS. Lily's probably already there." He glanced around to see if the boys were close, and then said, "Thanks for this, Night. Lily doesn't have a lot of female friends in Dallas."

"Don't mention it. She's your sister. She's family."

Tex leaned in, and we kissed. From somewhere down the alley, one of the two younger boys said, "Yuck." I climbed into the moving van and headed on my way.

Lily Banks, soon to be Lily Allen, was Tex's younger sister by five years. Their mother died when he was in high school, leaving behind him, his older brother who'd died in service, and Lily. Tex had been more of a father figure than a brother to her, which led to her seeing him as an authority figure to rally against. She married young and started her own family, determined not to repeat their mother's mistakes. Seventeen years and four boys later, she was facing life on her own for the first time in a *long* time, and in an about-face, she turned to Tex for help. It was a testament to his character that he never once questioned why it had taken so long for her to ask.

As an interior decorator with a modest skill set for renovations, I was a handy person to have on speed dial. When Lily first told Tex she was getting divorced, he offered to move her and the boys into his townhouse. As nice as his offer had been, it was impractical. Even my place, a sweet craftsman purchased for the cost of back taxes, didn't have the room for that much testosterone. But Lily's ex, who had originally resisted her repeated requests for a divorce, had a change of heart, offering his Dallas home as part of their settlement. Tex had been suspicious about the whole thing, but after a conversation about gift horses, even he recognized that one of his sister's biggest problems had been solved.

Lily's new house was an old one. Located in the Midway Hills neighborhood, a development north of Dallas Love Field airport, it was a classic mid-century ranch. It was closer to my house than Tex's, though not by much. Built in 1957, the house had never been renovated, which made it something of a unicorn. These days, developers were snapping up mid-century ranches at an alarming rate. My clients, lovers of mid-century modern style, used to hire me to decorate. Lately my job had expanded to include undoing the bland renovations completed by flippers in their misguided attempts to create neutral palettes. It had happened so frequently that I now offered a special rate for an undo/redo. My newest employee, a high school senior who showed far more promise as a contractor than a reporter (the job he held when I met him), was my secret weapon. He was eager to gain experience, and there was nothing like taking things apart to teach you how they were put together in the first place.

The drive to Midway Terrace from Tex's house took twenty-five minutes. I followed the directions and parked in front of a brick house with a massive oak tree in the front yard. Lily's car, a white hatchback, was parked in the driveway on the right. The back seat was packed with personal belongings she hadn't wanted to put in the truck.

The house was a sprawling ranch made of red brick and dark brown siding. Pinkish breeze blocks were stacked to the left and the right of the entrance. The house had a peaked roofline and clerestory windows to allow in natural light. In terms of mid-century modern, it was a divine example of architecture, and I couldn't wait to get inside to see what else I'd find.

I climbed down from the truck. A silver sportscar pulled into the driveway behind Lily's hatchback, and an attractive man got out. He wore a sport coat over a polo shirt and khakis, the uniform of the casual professional male. The man barely glanced my way before approaching an agitated woman who bore more than a passing resemblance to Tex.

"It's about time," the woman said.

"I don't have time for a whole scene, Lil. I've got a plane to catch."

"Right. It took you nine years, but now you're in a hurry?"

"The house is yours. Consider it a goodwill gesture." He dropped a set of keys into her open palm.

I would have recognized Lily even if this man hadn't used her name. She had the same coloring as Tex, dark blond hair and enough of a tan to appear healthy but not leathery. Her hair was pulled into a messy ponytail that tipped to the side on top of her head. I hadn't known what to expect from her —she *was* a born and bred Texas woman, and Tex had his own share of Lone Star State clichés imprinted on his DNA, but Lily seemed untouched by the Dallas beauty code. She wore an oversized white T-shirt and yoga pants with running shoes. I didn't know if anything about her was a trendy fashion choice or a function of her lifestyle. The one thing I didn't see in her was sadness.

By her interaction with the man, I guessed he was Gil, her soon-to-be ex-husband. He was halfway back to his car when Lily called out, "Don't you want to say goodbye to your boys?"

He stopped and turned. "They're here?" he asked

7

hopefully. He looked around the yard. Perspiration dotted his forehead, which struck me as odd, since it was a gorgeous seventy-five-degree day. There was something unusual about Gil, and his drive-by behavior wasn't the least of it. If Lily hadn't been waiting out front for him, I'd bet he would have left the keys in the mailbox, or worse—tossed them out the window onto the overgrown yard.

"No, they're not here. They're at my brother's place. If you wanted to see them, you could have agreed to help us move."

"Yeah, well, things happened pretty quickly." He glanced at his watch then over his shoulder. "I'd love to stay and chat, but I've gotta go."

"Fine," Lily said. "It's not like I expected anything else."

Lily turned her back on Gil, who speed-walked back to his car. His tires left skid marks on the street out front as he pulled away. I watched his taillights until they left the development.

I turned back to the house and discovered I wasn't the only person to watch the scene unfold. An older man with a gruff expression shook his head at the scene and then went into the house next door.

Lily had disappeared into the house. Instead of following her through the front door, I walked around the side, checking out the exterior until I reached the back patio.

Everything I'd heard about Gil was that he didn't want this divorce. Even though he and Lily had been separated for almost a decade, he refused every request to make that separation official. After the birth of their youngest, Gil moved to Dallas, taking a job as a botanical researcher at the Lakewood Arboretum. Lily maintained a separate life in

Austin, raising four boys on her own, working remotely as an executive assistant for a team of insurance brokers, and barely making ends meet.

Not until recently had Gil relented to her requests after landing a coveted job out of the country. Lily hadn't wanted to give him time to change his mind. She put her house on the market, and it sold quickly. Gil transferred the deed to a mid-century ranch to her name as part of their settlement, and here we were.

Lily hadn't said we were meeting anyone, but I heard her voice coming from inside the house. She was arguing with someone. Lily saw me outside the screen door and unlocked the door then gestured for me to come inside. I had to put my weight into it, but I finally got the door to slide open, catching the tail end of Lily's argument.

"—not what we agreed to," she said into her phone. "Maybe you did, but *I* didn't." She turned her back on me and wandered deeper into the house. "So help me, Gil. Don't do this. They're your boys too."

I knew from Tex that Lily's divorce was combative, but even so, I wandered away to give her privacy. The move wasn't entirely generous; I wanted to see the interior.

Lily went toward the right, so I went left. We'd been told the house was move-in ready, which was a vast overstatement. The carpet, once-white wall-to-wall shag, was stained in several places, and the light fixture, a seventies-era chandelier with plastic candles, dangled dangerously low. I left the living room and entered the kitchen, a study in black and white all the way up to a white ceiling with black polka dots. I was all for whimsy, but the effect agitated my nervous system and clashed with the slate tile flooring. Fixtures had been pulled away from the walls, exposing dirt and mouse traps, which were (fortunately) empty but spoke to a greater concern. Beyond the kitchen lay a den with black shag carpeting. You would think black carpet, while an unusual choice, would be effective in hiding signs of wear. You would be wrong. The carpet had faded to dark gray. The walls were bright white, and the smell indicated the paint was still fresh. I verified that assessment by dragging my fingertip along the paneling. The house was such a disaster that whitewashing one room was a slap in the face.

"Madison?" called Lily.

"In here," I said. "The room past the kitchen."

"My brother wasn't kidding," she said, hugging me. "You really do look just like Doris Day."

"The older I get, the less relevant that is. Your boys were more impressed with my ability to throw a baseball."

"You must have met Adam," she said. "He's my youngest. He doesn't go anywhere without that catcher's mitt." She held up her hands. "I'm not complaining. At least he forgot about snakes."

"He said he had a pet milk snake that got out of the terrarium."

She shook her head. "If by 'got out of his terrarium,' he meant 'got put into Mom's ten-pound bin of all-purpose flour,' then yes, that happened. And somehow, not one of my sons knows how a six-inch milk snake crawled across our house, climbed onto a counter, opened a cabinet, and climbed into a sealed bin of dry goods. I tell you, that snake could have sold tickets at the state fair if it had survived."

I liked her immediately. "I couldn't help overhearing you when I arrived. Were you talking to Gil again?"

She tossed her cell phone onto a torn red beanbag chair that had been left behind. "Yes, that was Gil. He agreed to hand over the keys to the house, but I knew when he dashed out of here there was going to be a problem. He claims he doesn't know anything about the condition of the interior. He said he hired a company to get it ready for us." She looked around. "If this is after the place was staged, imagine what it looked like before."

"Speaking of which, don't touch the walls. The paint is still wet."

Lily looked as if wet paint was too much to take. "I can't do this," she said. She dropped onto the red beanbag, and the fabric split, spewing foam pellets about a foot away from the seat. After glancing at the mess, she tipped her head back and closed her eyes. "Exactly how much can a person be expected to take?"

I assumed the question was rhetorical. "Why don't you wait here. I'll conduct a walk-through. If anything else needs to be handled, I'll make note of it."

"Thanks," she said.

I left her in the beanbag and checked the rest of the place out. I was both surprised and delighted to discover a pink bathroom complete with matching tub and a blue bathroom with a shower. A third bathroom, painted yellow and tiled in gray, sealed the deal. I could work wonders with this house if given the opportunity.

I found Lily where I'd left her. "It's not all bad," I said. "In fact, it's pretty great. Your ex might have thought he was burdening you with a massive fixer-upper, but he didn't factor in one thing."

"My never-ending capacity for struggle?"

"Your recent acquaintance with the owner of a company that remodels and redecorates mid-century modern houses." I gestured at the surroundings. "Lately I spend more time undoing what people like your ex think are upgrades. My team will check the structural integrity, which is probably in decent shape because these houses are indestructible. After that's cleared, it's a matter of decorating to your liking. I've got an entire inventory of furniture and fixtures, and you can have your pick of them at cost."

Lily sat up. "That's not fair." She attempted to stand, but the beanbag gave a good fight.

I held out my hand and pulled her to her feet.

She bent back down and grabbed her phone then pressed a number from her menu of recent calls. "Gil, it's Lily. I'm taking the house, but you're paying for upgrades. I hope your new job came with a healthy pay increase, because in addition to our divorce settlement, I'm sending you the bill."

CHAPTER TWO

LILY HUNG UP AND SHOVED HER PHONE INTO A POCKET ON THE side of her yoga pants. "Tonight, when I go to bed, I'm going to picture the expression on his face when he gets that message." She smiled. "I have a feeling I'll fall asleep happy for the first time in a long time."

Movement on the black carpet caught my eye. I looked down and saw a mouse race across the carpet and disappear into the bedroom. Lily saw it, too, and blanched.

"I'll handle that too," I said. I put my hand on her arm and steered her toward the front door. "But tonight, you're staying with me."

She parked her hatchback under the porte-cochère and we drove the moving truck to my place. I might not have the accommodation for four boys plus Tex, but my spare bedroom would be perfect for Lily. I gave her a moment to get what she needed from the truck while I checked in with Tex.

"Change of plans," I said. "The house needs work. Lily's going to stay with me tonight."

"This isn't an excuse to go to Magic Mike night at Jumbo's, is it?"

"You'll never know, will you?"

Tex's end of the phone went silent.

I quickly added, "It's nothing I can't handle, and I already told her I'd do the job at cost. I'll design around whatever she wants and bring in a team to handle any structural issues."

"You shouldn't take a financial hit over her ex-husband's passive-aggressive action."

"She already called her ex and told him he was paying."

"You sure you can fit this into your schedule?"

"Absolutely. I've just finished the last of four high-paying jobs that I never would have gotten if I didn't have a contractor on my payroll."

"Keep an eye on her, will you?" he asked. "I know that's a lot to ask, but I feel responsible. I should have seen this douchebag coming."

"Even if you did, there's not much you could have done about it. You can't make her do something she doesn't want to do, and you can't make her *not* do something she does. It's her life to live."

"Yes, but she's family. There are different rules."

I felt the familiar shock to the chest that came with the subject of family. More than half of my life had passed since my parents' death, but I still missed them. I made a living from obtaining the estates of recently deceased people of a certain age, amassing more inventory than I could use in one-off room remodels, but my parents' estate had sat, unexamined, in a storage facility in Pennsylvania. Not until last month, when the owner notified me that he was closing the facility and selling off unclaimed contents, was I faced with the need to do something with their belongings.

I'd come a long way from those days, when I worked at a resale shop alongside people who taught me about the design style I loved, but a part of me had gotten locked into that storage locker too. That part of me had sealed off, isolated from ever feeling that level of abandonment again.

"You there, Night?"

"I'm here," I said.

"Listen," he said, this time more gently. "I know this wasn't what you signed up for, and I promise I'll make it up to you. I've been looking out for Lily my whole life."

"You're a cop. You look out for everybody."

"Like I said, family is a whole different ball game."

Tex and I made plans for him to come to my house the next day, and I headed inside. Lily was in the Glenn Den, an astronaut-themed sitting room on the other side of the living room. Old houses generally had small footprints, especially ones with second floors. Even though Lily was two rooms away, I easily overheard her conversation.

"I can't. He's leaving the country. It's this or nothing, and I didn't go through all of this to end up with nothing. I can't put the boys through that."

She had her back turned to me. I hadn't tried to be quiet when I reentered the house, but she didn't appear to know I was there. I pulled two stemmed wineglasses out of a kitchen cabinet and then poured us each some white wine from a bottle I'd opened earlier in the week.

"You've already done enough," Lily said. "I can't expect you to keep on picking up the slack from my choices."

Ah, she must be talking to Tex. I put the wine away and prepped a charcuterie board with cheese, crackers, diced apples, jam, and honey and set everything on a laminated vintage TV tray. Then I added a couple of cocktail napkins with saucy (for 1960) expressions and carried the setup to her. The carpet silenced my footfalls. I set the tray on the coffee table and tapped Lily on the shoulder.

She jumped. Her eyes moved from mine to the tray. She said, "I have to go. I'll call you tomorrow." She disconnected and thrust the phone into her pocket. "Keds and carpet." She pointed at my feet. "Stealthy combination."

"One of the many benefits to spending life in sneakers." I handed her a wineglass. "Is he going to be okay with the boys tonight?"

"Who?"

"Tex," I said. I pointed at her pocket. "I overheard part of your conversation and assumed you were talking to him."

"Sure, of course. The boys love him, and honestly, they could use a strong male role model after having Gil as their dad."

When Tex and I first met, the last thing I would have called him was a strong role model. For a moment, I rolled that memory around in my mind and smiled to myself. But regardless of Tex's reputation, he was dependable, honest, hard-working, and fair, and I couldn't really imagine anyone else I'd want in my life if I had to raise four boys of varying ages.

"He's been looking forward to your visit," I said. I gestured to the sofa. We both sat.

"They're probably knee-deep in video games and

popcorn by now." Lily held out her wineglass and we clinked. "To having the night off."

"You deserve it."

Considering we'd met for the first time a few hours ago, Lily and I got along well. We put a dent in the charcuterie spread and finished the wine, which came as a surprise when she tipped the bottle upside down to shake out the last few drops. Maybe she wasn't the only one who needed a night off.

She stretched her arms overhead and yawned. "I know it's early, but I'm sacked. Would you mind if I turn in for the night?"

I glanced at the clock mounted on the wall behind her. It was a little after nine. I was a morning person by nature, having maintained a morning lap-swimming regimen for the better part of a decade. Between my regular routine and half a bottle of wine, I was whipped too.

"Sure," I said. "Sleep as long as you want tomorrow morning. We can meet Tex for breakfast and come up with a plan then."

We took turns in the shower, me going first. I was half-asleep by the time her shower ended. In the hallway, I heard the linen closet opening and closing and then creaking hardwood as she walked to the spare bedroom. Rocky, my caramel and white Shih-Tzu, lay on the foot of the bed, curled up in a messy fluff of fur that was desperate for a trim. A few weeks ago he'd caught his paw under the rails of a rocking chair and had spent his recovery time being carried around in a handbag.

Headlights from a passing car lit up the windows, and

Rocky raised his head. He stared at the window and, as the light faded, rested his head on his paw.

I wasn't used to having a houseguest other than Tex, and when he stayed over, he didn't use the guest room. Old houses came with interesting noises, and tonight, I heard them all. I eventually drifted off around eleven thirty.

At quarter to one, I woke with a start. Another set of headlights danced against the glass of my bedroom windows. I pulled the covers over my head and rolled over, catching the tail end of sleep before it slipped away for good.

The next morning, my internal alarm woke me at a quarter after five. I'd long ago learned the rest of the world didn't function on my schedule, so I gave Lily ample time to sleep in and took Rocky out for a walk. Then I discovered the first problem of the day.

* * *

"She's gone," I said to Tex on an early morning phone call.

"She can't be gone."

"I'm telling you, she's not here. The truck's gone too." I poured a cup of yesterday's coffee and set my mug in the microwave.

"Did you try to call her?"

"I called you. I thought maybe she missed the boys and went to your place."

"Walk me through your night."

"There's not much to walk through," I said. "After your call, we sat around talking like a couple of women who hadn't had time to sit around talking. We finished off a bottle of wine and then went to bed."

"After what call?"

"Last night when you called her. Maybe she called you. I overheard part of the conversation while I prepped a cheese board." I wandered to the door and let Rocky out. I sat on my stoop while he trotted slowly toward his favorite tree.

"What is it with women and cheese boards? Did Giada do a special or something?"

"I'm pretty sure you've watched more Giada specials than I do."

"You're right. Bad reference." He gave the conversation a moment. "Did the History Channel run a special on Julia Child?"

Ooooooh! "Are you not concerned with the absence of your sister?"

"I'm more concerned with this phone call she was on. I was outside playing catch with Adam and Gabe. What did she say that made you think it was me?"

I thought back to the snippets of conversation I'd overheard. "I was trying to give her space. I didn't think I needed to eavesdrop so soon after meeting her." As I stood outside and watched Rocky, the white moving truck turned the corner and drove toward me. I watched as the driver parked alongside my front hedges. The driver's-side door opened, and a few seconds later, Lily walked around the front of the truck, holding a tray with coffee cups.

"Good morning," she called out cheerily. "I couldn't find your coffee, and I didn't want to wake you."

I stared at her. *She* didn't want to wake *me*? At five thirty in the morning? Who was this woman?

"Is that Lily?" Tex asked.

"Yes."

"Don't tell her you're on the phone with me." He hung up.

I'd been curious about Tex's relationship with his sister, and not just because of the glimpse it might give me into the boy he was before he became a man. Tex was in control. All the time. Even when he'd been under suspicion of murder, suspended from the police force while an internal investigation was conducted, he'd never seen himself as a victim. He simply found a different way to do what he did, which was to discover the solution from a fresh perspective.

But asking me to pretend I hadn't called him about her felt different. Tex had already told me he'd watched out for Lily their whole life. They had a falling out after he was left with the weighty decision of taking his mother off life support two months after she'd had a stroke. It was the worst possible eighteen-year-old birthday present a boy could get: Congratulations, now you're her legal guardian. Sign this paperwork.

I knew that decision had helped propel Tex from boy to man. I knew losing his older brother had affected him too. And I knew Lily had been thirteen at the time, a girl who still needed her mother even if that mother was a drunk who set a bad example with a revolving door of suitors. But other than that, I didn't know much else about them.

I tucked my phone into the patch pocket of my blue and white knit dress. It came from the estate of Kelley Hawks, a former saleslady for Tiche Goettinger's department store in Arlington. Along with her meticulously maintained wardrobe I'd found a stash of postcards with images of the store. They'd been addressed and stamped but never sent. The message on each was the same: *My new employer!* Her enthusiasm over having landed the glamorous job was evident and I always wondered what had happened to Kelley to keep her from sending the postcards to everyone she knew.

I accepted a cup of coffee from Lily, then led her and Rocky back into my kitchen. "I guess my efforts to let you sleep in were wasted," I said.

Lily looked at me and took a sip of her coffee. She shrugged. "You're right. When I talked to my brother last night, he told me not to worry, but I couldn't help myself."

That's funny, I thought. According to Tex, that phone call hadn't been to him.

CHAPTER THREE

I PLACED ROCKY IN A WICKER TOTE BAG AND CARRIED HIM TO my vintage Alfa Romeo. It wasn't the most convenient car to use for a move, but until we worked out where Lily was going to stay, it didn't seem wise to burn up gas driving around in the moving truck. I drove us to Tex's townhouse. Traffic was just starting to show signs of life. That was one of the benefits of getting up early. We made good time and parked outside Tex's garage twenty minutes later.

Lily and I walked around to the front door with Rocky peeking his fluffy head out of the tote. Knowing Tex's place was infested with boys, I rang the bell instead of letting myself in like usual.

We waited upwards of a minute before I rang it again.

And again.

The third time turned out to be the charm. Footsteps pounded down the staircase, thundering like a small army on the other side of the door. Voices argued. "Don't tell Mom!"

Lily and I shared a glance. She rapped her knuckles on the door. "Don't tell Mom what?" she asked.

The sounds on the other side of the door went quiet. Then someone said, "Uh-oh."

The lock clunked and the doorknob turned. Gabe and Adam stood on the other side. Neither boy was tall enough to see through the peephole and know who was on our side. A small Shi Chi dog, Wojo, yipped at us from the floor. It was a lot of energy to be packed on the three-foot square tile landing directly inside Tex's entrance.

"What have I told you about opening the door to strangers?" Lily asked.

"We knew it was you," Gabe said. "We recognized your voice."

"He has a point," I told Lily.

I lifted Rocky from his tote, and he greeted Wojo with some butt-sniffing. Lily turned Adam around. We followed him and Gabe back up the steps. The boys gained speed with the dogs leading the way. Lily and I followed at a more respectable pace. Any questions about what they didn't want to tell Mom were answered when we found Tex in his living room, holding a bag of ice against his face.

"What happened to you?" Lily asked.

"It was an accident," Adam said. He looked up at his mom, all wide-eyed innocence and sweetness. Her eyebrows rose, and she turned her attention back to Tex.

He lowered the ice, revealing a purplish-magenta bruise and swelling around his eye socket. "I was giving Adam tips on how to improve his swing." He grinned, letting us both know he saw the humor in the situation, even if he'd been on the wrong end of the punch line.

I reached out and brushed my hands against the side of his face. He flinched. As funny as it was, it still looked like it hurt. "When did this happen?"

"Last night."

"You didn't"—I started, but Tex shook his head ever so slightly— "have to go to the emergency room, did you?"

"Not much you can do about a black eye except ice it," he said.

I took the bag from his hand and carried it to the kitchen. The townhouse floor plan had an open kitchen that faced the living room, and from my position behind the sink, I could easily watch Lily, Tex, and the two boys.

"Where are David and George?" Lily asked.

"I sent them to the grocery store to pick up steaks."

"It's seven in the morning."

"You've never seen steak and eggs on a breakfast menu?"

Lily shook her head. "Are you going to be a good influence on them?"

"Better than the last one."

It wasn't hard to see that Tex and Lily had a typical sibling relationship. I felt like I was intruding on their squabble, so I dumped the ice bag's partially melted contents into the sink as a reminder that I was still there. Tex glanced at me, but Lily didn't. I busied myself by refilling the bag with a fresh handful of ice cubes.

The front door opened, and a new male voice called up the stairs. "Uncle Tex? Somebody parked in your driveway."

"That's me," I called back.

Footsteps pounded up the stairs, slower and more deliberate than those of the younger boys. David, the lanky teen I'd seen behind the wheel of Tex's Jeep yesterday, carried a full shopping bag up the stairs and set it on the kitchen counter. He spotted me first, but his mom was a close second. She put her hands on her hips.

"Were you here when this happened?" she asked him.

A second boy, younger than David but older than Adam and Gabe, came up the stairs, carrying two net bags bulging with additional groceries. "Give Adam a break, Mom," he said. "Shit happens."

"George! Watch your language."

George shrugged. He set the grocery bags on the counter and picked Wojo up. To the easily excited Wojo, this was like heaven. He wriggled free and ran around, yapping at ankles near and far, vying for his slice of attention. Rocky sat under a dining room chair, taking it all in.

I slid open a drawer, pulled out two dog biscuits, then came around the side of the sink and gave one to Rocky. Wojo raced over to me and took the other one. Briefly, all eyes focused on the dogs as they attacked their biscuit. The silence that draped over the moment was a nice reprieve from the chaos that had existed since we arrived, and I had a feeling Wojo would run a lot of interference after we left.

"George, David, take the groceries up to the roof," Tex instructed. "There's a fridge up there. We'll cook them in a bit."

"Can we go with?" Gabe asked.

"We're all going," Lily said. She put her hand on Adam's shoulders and turned him around so he faced the staircase. She pointed. "Go."

Wojo and Rocky led the charge.

Once Tex and I were alone again, I carried the bag of ice back to him. He held out his hand, but before I handed the bag over, I cocked my head to the side and assessed his face. "Makes you look sexy."

"I thought I already looked sexy."

"No, you already looked arrogant. This takes it down a notch." I gently held the plastic bag against his face. "Besides, there's no way this is your first black eye."

"First time it was caused by a ten-year-old." He grinned.

"I'm not going to ask who delivered the others. I can easily picture a steady stream of criminals, ex-girlfriends, and husbands getting in line."

Tex reached up and placed his warm hand over mine on the ice bag. The contact felt good, a bit of intimacy in a temporarily overcrowded house of people who had more of a claim on his attention than I did.

"Speaking of husbands," Tex said, expertly diverting attention from a discussion of his bachelor days, "what happened yesterday with Gil?"

I pulled my hand out from under his and joined him on his black leather sofa. A knee injury kept me from tucking one leg under the other, so I sat sideways and stretched my leg out so the sole of my foot touched him. He picked up my foot and rested it on top of his leg.

"I've officially joined the team that thinks Gil is a jerk," I said. "The house he left your sister is unlivable."

Tex's face clouded. "He said it was move-in ready."

"Maybe for the mouse that ran through the living room, it was, but otherwise, it's a mess. At least one window was broken, and the interior is, shall we say, outdated and not in a good way."

Tex's eyebrows pulled together as he tried to process what that meant. "Your whole business model is based on outdated interiors. What do you mean by 'not in a good way'?"

"Black shag carpet with bleach stains. Polka-dotted ceilings in a room with shale tile floors."

Tex stared at me for a stretch. I couldn't read his thoughts. Usually, that meant he was thinking about police matters. In this case, I suspected those thoughts involved Gil, but I doubted Tex was thinking about issuing Gil a citation. "Can you do anything with it?" he finally asked.

"I'll go over the place to check for structural damage and bring in an electrical team to make sure the wiring is up to code. An exterminator can handle the mouse situation. Once those things are done, the rest is cosmetic. I already told Lily she'll get the house of her dreams at cost."

"It's a job like any other job," Tex said. "Sounds like it'll take you away from your regular business. You shouldn't lose money over this."

"She's your sister."

"Yeah, but Gil knew what he was doing when he offered her that house. He can't get away with this." Tex dropped the bag of ice onto the sofa and moved my foot from his leg. Then he stood and picked up his Jeep keys from a bowl by the door.

"Where are you going?"

"The arboretum. Gil's supposed to meet Lily later this morning, and I'm going in her place."

I stood too. "Is that a good idea? I know your instincts are to look out for her, but she'll feel better about this if *she* handles it, not you."

Tex dangled his keys from his index finger. Despite what I'd said, the black eye made him look menacing. It didn't matter who had inflicted it, though the story that it had been a ten-year-old-boy didn't help. Tex would not have his usual commanding presence.

"Besides, that shiner makes you look a little...rough around the edges."

"I thought you said I looked sexy?"

"I was being polite." I took the keys from his hand and placed them back in the bowl. "I'll go with Lily. Moral support. She needs to stand on her own, and that will be easier if she doesn't have you to stand there for her."

"Fine," he said. "I'll watch the boys."

"Are you sure you're safe with them?"

"We got the worst of it out of the way already. The rest of this visit will be a cakewalk."

* * *

LILY, Rocky, and I arrived at the Lakewood Arboretum shortly after nine. The grounds, consisting of sixty-six acres of landscaped and cultivated plant life, gardens available for rent for private parties, and public areas for picnics, were a bright spot amongst Dallas's growing concrete footprint. Researchers whose work was contained on the property conducted ongoing experiments that led to advancements in horticulture, and more than one Dallas bride had said "I do" in one of the gardens.

Gil worked in one of the research facilities. I didn't fully understand what it was he did, only that his work had landed him a high-paying job in New Zealand and after years of ignoring Lily's requests for a divorce, he finally seemed to want his own fresh start. I didn't understand people who clung to the dysfunctional parts of their lives, but I was possibly the minority. After the person I thought was my future told me he was married, I'd broken all ties and moved seven states away. (I took the scenic route.) So much had changed in my life since then that standing face-to-face with him at the top of a ski slope was a distant memory. The knee injury I'd sustained after skiing away and hitting a patch of ice never quite let me fully forget.

Lily flipped down the visor in the passenger seat. Vanity mirrors weren't standard issue in sixties-era Alfa Romeos, but I'd long ago clipped a round mirror on for lipstick emergencies. She touched up her Barbie-pink shade and then dabbed at her lips with a tissue.

"Are you ready for this?" I asked.

"Honestly? No. I'm so angry I don't even want to see him. I want this all to be over, but I know this won't go easily. No matter what he told me about handing over the papers, there's going to be a hitch. There always is. Look at what happened with the house."

"You have control over what happens today," I said.

"Do I? I've been asking for a divorce for over nine years, and now he's leaving the country. If I don't jump, I might never get him to sign those papers. I can't believe after all this time of trying to get him to give me back my life, I'm at his beck and call. It's a shitty situation."

I stifled a smile.

She caught my expression and smiled too. "Oh, please. If

the worst habit my boys pick up is the occasional swear word, I'll be a happy mother."

"I tell you what. You wait here with Rocky. I'll go inside and get the papers. You don't need to interact with him at all. If he asks where you are, I'll tell him you didn't think it was necessary to say goodbye in person."

Lily glanced at me. "That would really burn him up." She smiled.

"Then it's settled."

Lily told me where to find Gil's research lab. I left the keys in the ignition and consulted a map of the arboretum grounds. The walk was short, and along the way, I passed a tour group of seniors. I recognized one from the pool where I usually swam laps each morning, and I waved hello but didn't stop to chat. I was a woman on a mission.

I found a building marked Herbology at the end of the path. The door was open, and a breeze pushed it in as if welcoming me. I entered.

The spicy smell of herbs filled the room. Tables that held collections of plants were lined up in long rows. At the end of the room stood two desks, two computers, and two chairs. One monitor glowed blue, and the other one was dark.

"Gil?" I called out. "Gil Banks? I'm here for Lily." There was no answer.

A growing anxiety rose within me. Something about this meeting didn't feel right, and I'd been in enough didn't-feel-right situations by now to trust my gut.

I walked deeper into the herbarium toward the desks. I found a bulging envelope with Lily's name on it propped against one of the computer monitors. The contents weren't my business, so I slipped the envelope into my handbag and turned to leave.

Then I saw the body on the arboretum floor. It wasn't until I got closer that I recognized Gil. His skin was a purplish-white hue, and his eyes were glassy and unfocused. His mouth was open, a small, round O in the middle of a vacant, lifeless face.

CHAPTER FOUR

I CHECKED GIL'S PULSE AS A TECHNICALITY. THERE WAS NO
visible murder weapon, no visible wound, but that was a job
for the medical examiner. Gil was dead.

Other observations came quickly after that: the door to
his lab being open, the envelope of divorce papers with Lily's
name prominently displayed on his desk. Whoever had killed
him knew Lily was coming here to meet him and that
someone was stacking the deck against her in terms of
suspicious behavior.

Normally, my first call would be to the police. But Tex
was the police, and Lily was Tex's sister. And Lily was right
outside, and I was caught in a storm of indecision.

I went with my gut and called Tex. The call went to
voicemail. I tried two more times. It wasn't like him not to
answer, but I also didn't know what four boys would do to
Tex's habits.

A phone rang from somewhere near Gil's body. I froze, as
if this dead man were going to come back to life to take the

call. I saw the phone screen, illuminated, next to his hip. The number wasn't programmed, and before I thought too much about it, I typed it into my phone and hit the green button to initiate a call. Gil's phone stopped ringing. My call dropped, but a moment later, an incoming call rang from the same number. I stared at the phone for too long, and the call went to my voicemail.

While I stood over Gil's body, I heard my name. I looked up and saw Lily in the doorway.

"What's taking so long?" she asked. She had Rocky cradled against her chest.

"Lily." I turned around and looked at Gil's body. "Wait in the car. I'll be out in a moment."

My protective instincts kicked in. I tore a blank square from a paper cube on the desk and wrote my address on it then went outside, where Lily was waiting right by the door. I handed her the paper.

"This is my address. Use your phone's GPS, go to my house, and wait for me there. Please don't ask any questions."

"What's wrong?" Lily asked, ignoring my instructions. "Didn't Gil give you the paperwork?" She pushed past me and stormed into the room. "I swear to God, Gil, I'm going to kill you."

"Lily!" I cried out, but she ignored that too. I chased after her, too late to keep her from seeing what I had. I found her standing over Gil's body, her shoulders sloped and her hands balled in tight fists.

I couldn't imagine how Lily felt, standing next to the spouse she'd held anger toward for a decade, the spouse who prevented her from moving on with her life after acknowledging that she'd made a poor choice when she married him. I couldn't imagine what emotions she felt: sadness at his loss of life? Anger that she'd never get to tell him off? Relief that she was free? Guilt that she felt relief? I wouldn't judge her for any of them. Her marriage had been complicated, but it had come to an unexpected end. Anybody would feel a maelstrom of emotions after this.

She kicked Gil's body. It shifted slightly. "You jerk," she said under her breath. "I can't believe you did this to me." A ragged breath escaped her mouth as her lungs hitched. I put my hands on her upper arms and pulled her away from him.

"You need to leave," I said. "Go to my place and wait for me there."

Whether because of my insistence or my expression, Lily acquiesced. She nodded, turned, and left. I followed her to the exit and watched as she set Rocky on the passenger-side seat, climbed into the driver's seat, and drove away before I went back inside.

Under any other circumstances, I would know what to do. But this time, I didn't. Common sense told me the police needed to be notified, the crime scene needed to be contained, and the body needed to be taken off the premises and sent to the morgue for an autopsy. Calling 9-1-1 was the right thing to do. But getting Lily mixed up in a homicide would complicate her new life and put Tex in a bad situation. Would he understand if I put his sister in those crosshairs? And wasn't it worse that she'd been here but I'd sent her away?

Rationally, Tex would understand if I followed standard procedure. His respect for the penal system was unimpeachable. But emotionally... I didn't know. I'd never seen Tex around Lily before. To date, the only family of his

I'd met was his cousin who ran a tow yard in Dallas, and I wasn't even sure if they were related by blood. Lily and the boys were the only nuclear family Tex had, which was not a lot but was more than I had.

My memory flashed on the cartons that had arrived from the storage locker in Pennsylvania where I'd stored my parents' estate after they died. I'd had help unloading the cartons into my satellite office then avoided opening them because they reminded me of the last time I had a family. The sadness and grief over their loss that I hadn't dealt with for thirty years was banging on my door. Ultimately, while I could do nothing about me, I could do something about Lily. I could shelter her from this. I just needed to get a burner phone to report Gil's murder anonymously and let the police arrive and investigate. There was no reason for Lily to get involved.

I called Tex again. He answered on the first ring. "Night," he said, "I talked to Lily. She told me what happened."

Waves of relief cascaded over me. "Did she ask what we should do?"

"There's nothing to do. Get the divorce papers and leave Gil there."

I held the phone away from my head, checked to make sure I'd called the right number, then pulled the phone back. "Are you sure? I thought you'd tell me to—"

"I have to go." Tex disconnected.

I stared at the phone. Nobody was acting the way they normally acted. When I glanced down at my handbag to make sure the divorce papers were still there, I saw a dirty footprint on the floor. I stepped backward and another footprint appeared. I spotted a roll of paper towels sitting next to the messy desks and stepped around Gil's body to retrieve them. I forgot all about the paper towels when I noticed a sticker on the corner of the window. It was for a local, privately owned security company called Big Bro.

A host of thoughts flooded my mind. If the lab was being surveilled as part of a security package, then there would be a record of whatever had happened here. I knew Big Bro's owner, so my next move had nothing to do with paper towels. I covered my hand with my sleeve to keep from leaving any evidence of my presence, picked up the phone on the desk, and called the number on the sticker.

"What is it now?" a female voice asked.

I recognized the voice, but until I said something, she had no way of knowing I, not Gil, was calling her.

"Donna?" I paused. "It's Madison. Do you service a security contract at the Lakewood Arboretum?" I asked.

"Yes. Why?"

I turned and looked at the floor. Gil's motionless body lay mere feet away. "There's been a security breach," I told her. "If this is your account, you need to get here now." I hung up before she could ask me any questions.

Donna Nast—Nasty, as she'd come to be known—was a former police officer who'd once been romantically linked to Tex. She left the force and started her own private security company, quickly exploiting one of the biggest growth sectors in Dallas and making a name for herself in the process. She'd been named one of Dallas's 30 Entrepreneurs to Watch, though ironically, with her security cameras mounted at the hottest spots around town, she was more likely the one watching us.

Nasty and I had started out on rocky footing, but we'd

reached a level of professional respect that almost bordered on friendliness. I could count on her in an emergency (and had on more than one occasion), and I thought she'd say the same thing about me. We were opposites from head (long, professionally colored copper hair streaked with highlights versus Doris Day ash blond) to toe (red-soled Louboutin stilettos versus Keds), but in many ways, we were more alike than not.

Nasty arrived within minutes. "Madison?" she called out.

In the convex mirror hanging in the corner of the lab, I watched Nasty stride toward me. I turned away from the mirror and walked toward her with my hands up. "I wouldn't go any farther."

"Don't act so freaked out, Madison. You didn't do anything wrong. Gil Banks trips his silent alarm once a week."

I lowered my hands and looked around, though I knew by definition, a silent alarm would be undetectable. "How do you know?"

"This is one of my accounts."

"Did you see what happened here?"

"No cameras. This is privately funded research. Gil trips that alarm so often I gave him the codes to reset it. When you called, I assumed it was him." Her face clouded. "Why did you call from his desk?"

It seemed unusual that Nasty, a smart and savvy businesswoman who'd built Big Bro herself after leaving the police force, had gotten so frustrated by one of her clients that she handed over the reset codes to him. Considering that a dead body lay behind me, though, I didn't waste time inquiring about her choice to handle the problem on her own. Her near proximity when I called could probably be explained by her already being on her way, so I didn't ask about that either.

Nasty showed greater loyalty to her clients than to the law. Usually, but not always, those two were on the same side, but until I knew how she'd react to the current situation, I was in unfamiliar territory.

"I need your help. Actually, Tex needs your help. Actually, Tex's sister needs your help."

"Spit it out, Madison."

"Tex's sister's soon-to-be-ex-husband is dead on the floor behind me." Some sentences just never sound right, even if they're true.

Nasty stared at me. I assumed it was because she didn't understand the connections I'd made. I stepped aside to give her a clear view of Gil's body.

She shifted her attention from me to him. Finally, she asked, "Did you call the police?"

"Not yet. I know I should. I just thought—"

"Don't."

"Good. Okay. Tex said the same thing, but—I guess it doesn't matter. I came here with his sister, but I sent her to my place in my car. If you give me a ride to the closest cell phone store, I'll buy a burner and call this in anonymously."

Something I said got Nasty's attention. She looked back up at me. "Lily was here?" she asked.

"Yes. Do you know her?"

"Yes." When Nasty didn't offer any additional details, I realized that the two of them might have been friends. I wasn't prone to jealousy, especially over Tex's past relations, but suddenly, I felt insecure. I pushed the inconvenient emotion aside, knowing it was far from the most important issue of the morning.

Nasty's unexpected arrival had been reassuring at first, but the longer we stood in the arboretum with a dead body, the more I questioned *why* Nasty wasn't advising me to follow protocol.

"We have to do something," I said.

She came closer and stared at Gil's body. "You said this was Lily's husband?"

"Yes. You never met him?"

"I met him but not through her. When I met her, she was separated. This guy was a real prince," she said, though her tone indicated he was anything but. "His account is separate from the arboretum. He demanded I sign a confidentiality clause and service the contract myself. After too many false reports, I make him write me a penalty check every time he trips the system. This way saves me gas. When that call came in, the last person I expected to be on the other end of the phone was you."

"Sorry to disappoint."

"I never said it was a disappointment."

We stood there staring at Gil's body on the floor. I hadn't called 9-1-1, which seemed the obvious next course of action. I pulled my sleeve back down over my hand, lifted the receiver, and then stopped. I already knew what would happen once I made that call. The police would tell me to wait at the scene, and when they arrived, they'd scour the place, collect evidence, and get my statement. They'd find out I'd been here with Lily. They'd discover the silent alarm had tripped but Nasty hadn't responded. They'd take the divorce papers, and Lily would be trapped in the same limbo she'd been living in for the past nine-plus years.

And then the investigating detectives would easily determine Lily was the most likely suspect to have committed this crime, especially after they learned of the derelict ranch Gil had left her. I could provide an alibi for Lily, though I couldn't explain what happened when she took the truck and left this morning. And when the police found out about that, they'd have just about everything they needed.

She was Tex's sister.

Tex's *family*.

She was a mother of four who finally had a chance at a fresh start after being held in place for far too long. And as I stood there with Nasty, staring at Lily's husband's unmoving body, I knew what to do.

I turned to Nasty. "Who else knows about the alarm?"

"Nobody."

I nodded. "Will you give me a ride?"

"Let's go."

CHAPTER FIVE

IT WASN'T EVERY DAY I LEFT A CRIME SCENE.

Something about sitting in the passenger seat of Nasty's Saab as we pulled out of the parking lot and onto Garland Road made me feel less like Doris Day and more like half of Thelma and Louise. Neither Nasty nor I had done anything wrong, but a low-level anxiety remained in place even as we put distance between us and the body that lay on the arboretum floor. With each decision I made, my actions were becoming less explainable as above-the-law choices, and Nasty's compliance just blurred the line between right and wrong more. But surely someone would discover Gil's body sooner rather than later.

The car ride back to Tex's townhouse was silent. Nasty rolled down her window and allowed the cool, passing wind to blow her hair away from her face. Leaving the crime scene felt wrong, but so did too many other things, and almost all of them involved Lily. Tex had looked out for her for most of her life, but this time, he'd left that responsibility to me.

Except Gil had been about to leave the country to start a new job.

Did that mean something? It certainly felt relevant, especially now, knowing Gil wasn't going to make his flight.

I glanced at Nasty out of the corner of my eye. For someone who'd worked for the police, she seemed remarkably unconcerned with our actions. That, too, gave the morning a surreal haze, like watching events through gossamer. From having a roommate last night to finding a body this morning, nothing about today felt real.

Nasty parked in Tex's driveway. His garage door was open, and the Jeep was inside. I led the way through the back door, which opened onto the downstairs guest bedroom. The single bed was a pile of unmade sheets, and David, the oldest boy, had left his clothes from yesterday in a pile on the floor. Nasty and I passed through the room, climbed the stairs, and found Adam on the sofa, playing a video game. David was perched on a stool, texting someone. George was in the kitchen filling a glass with Coke, and as soon as he looked at Nasty, the bottle of Coke slipped from his hand and fell. Brown soda chugged out onto the floor. George's face turned bright red.

"Clean it up before Uncle Tex comes out," David said without looking up from his phone.

George picked up the bottle and set it on the counter. He fumbled with a roll of paper towels, tore off about half of the roll, and then bent back down and mopped up the spill. I glanced at Nasty. She seemed unfazed.

A toilet flushed, and a few seconds later, Tex came out. His face was grayer than usual, and his hair was damp. His black eye had blossomed to a full spectrum of colors: purple and magenta, tinged with yellow and green. He held up his finger and took the glass of Coke from George, swallowed a few gulps, and then set it on the counter.

"Are you..." My voice drifted off as I took in the sight of Tex. "...okay?"

"Now's not the time," he said. "Where's Lil?"

"I sent her to my place."

"Did she get the papers?"

"I have them." I pulled the envelope out of my handbag and waved it back and forth. "I'll give them to her when I get there."

"You left Gil there, right?"

The question was unusual, all things considered. I glanced at Nasty. She leaned on the counter, her phone in her hands. George, having sort of cleaned up the mess he'd made, screwed the cap back onto the bottle of Coke and put it into the refrigerator. Then he came around behind Nasty and checked out her butt. Tex stifled a smile.

"Can I talk to you alone?" I asked.

Instead of answering, he turned and went back into the bathroom.

"Is he okay?" I asked David.

David looked up from his phone. "Gabe put a laxative on his steak."

Adam set off in a fit of giggles.

"Where is Gabe?" I asked.

"Upstairs," David said. "Uncle Tex told him to clean the grill until it looked like it just came off the factory floor."

The toilet flushed again. When Tex came out this time, he held a wet towel to his forehead. "I think I'm coming down with something."

Nasty looked up. "Sounds like a case of the trots."

"Who squealed?" Tex asked the room. He tossed the wet towel onto the counter and shook his head. "Do you mind keeping Lily company for today?" he asked me. "I hate to ask, but after what she went through this morning, I don't think she should be alone."

"You talked to her?"

"No, but seeing Gil under those conditions—that couldn't have been easy." Tex turned pale green and returned to the bathroom.

"How long has he been like this?" I asked George. He didn't seem to hear me, since all of his attention was now focused on Nasty. I really didn't think I would be getting in the way of blossoming love, so I moved directly in front of George and blocked his chances of initiating a conversation with her. He tried to look around me and then realized I knew what he was doing.

"What?" George asked.

"How long has Uncle Tex been sick?" I asked.

"He's been in the bathroom for most of the morning."

"Have you talked to your mom?"

"Yeah. She called about an hour ago and asked if we were behaving."

"Did she talk to Uncle Tex?"

"He was in the bathroom."

"Did you tell her what Gabe did?"

"Uncle Tex told us not to. He said if anybody said anything, we were eating celery for dinner." He looked at David. "Thanks a lot, bro."

The bathroom opened and Tex came back out. The top button of his jeans was open, and he held his hand to his stomach. He glanced at the glass of Coke on the counter but didn't drink any.

"I think it's best I stay home today," Tex said to me. Nasty stood off to the side, listening in. "Keep an eye on Lily, would you? After all this time, she deserves a clean break. I don't want her getting mixed up in what happened today."

I picked up the towel, ran icy water over it, then held it up to Tex's forehead. Even with his unexpected bathroom issues, he was choosing his words carefully around the boys, which hinted at how far he'd go to protect them. He wasn't the kind of guy who played the victim, but after twenty-four hours with Lily's boys, he looked as if he'd already been through the wringer.

"Don't worry about your sister. I need to go into the studio, but I'll take Lily with me and find something for her to do."

Nasty interrupted me. "Is she any good with computers?"

"Why?"

Nasty shrugged. "My tech guy quit," she said. She glanced at me, and I sensed her asking me to go along with her. "I could give her some temp work if she can handle it, but I don't have time to babysit."

"I'd rather she wasn't left alone today," Tex said. He turned his attention back to me.

"Lily can work with me at Mad for Mod. I'll have her start going through my inventory to see what she'd like in the house."

Tex nodded, as if my proposal was the suitable solution he'd been waiting for. "You need a ride back to—" He closed his eyes for a moment. "I've got to be empty by now."

"You stay here," Nasty said. "I'll give Madison a ride back to her place."

Tex nodded and went back into the bathroom.

Nasty and I left. Tex's predicament might have played a role in his choice to protect family over proper police procedure, but since his predicament came from family, I'd expect his loyalties had been tested. I climbed back into Nasty's Saab, and we were halfway to my house before she spoke.

"You've got a problem," she said.

"Keeping Lily busy isn't a problem," I said. "I already told her I'd redecorate the house her husband left her, so having her go through my inventory will give me an idea of what she'd like."

"Not that." She cut her eyes from the road to me and then back to the road. "Tex doesn't know Gil's dead."

"Of course he knows. He said he didn't want her to get mixed up in what happened. He doesn't want her to be alone today. You were standing right there—how did you not hear that?"

She sighed. "I'm not going to pretend I know Tex the man better than you, but I do know Tex the cop better than you. I worked with him, remember? That man wouldn't be so cavalier about you or his sister fleeing a crime scene."

"We didn't exactly flee—"

"You gave Lily your car keys and told her to leave, didn't you?"

"Yes, but—"

"And after I arrived, we left without notifying the authorities."

"Yes, but—"

"And to date, we haven't called the police."

"At your suggestion!"

"It was what's best for me. You already know that's how I make my decisions."

"What if I'd said I was going to call it in? Would you have tried to stop me?"

"You didn't call it in, so we'll never know, will we?" She flashed me a smile, and then her expression turned serious. "Don't worry. I'll handle it."

That idea might have worried me more.

For the duration of the short drive, I reminded myself that Nasty was a celebrated member of the community, a successful businessperson, a trusted acquaintance, and a mother. I doubted she'd risk all of that over a shady botanist.

We rounded the corner of the street where I lived, and Nasty pulled up behind an unfamiliar red Lexus with a sticker on the back windshield that said Lakewood Prep Academy. The Lexus was parked behind my Alfa Romeo, which was parked behind Lily's moving truck. It was beginning to look like a block party.

I started to get out of Nasty's car when she put her hand on my arm to stop me.

"I didn't tell you the truth about why I showed up today," she said. "Gil never demanded that I service his policy personally. That was the fourth time there's been a crime at one of my accounts in the past month, and I'm losing business. I've had to lay off some of my staff and start servicing calls myself."

"You can't pick up the slack on your own."

"I didn't lie about how often Gil tripped the alarm. He

was pretty clueless when it came to that. I reset the alarm when I got there this morning."

"If you gave Gil the reset codes, the police may assume he reset them himself."

"That's not the problem." With both hands, she pushed her hair away from her face. "The alarm went off again while we were talking to Tex."

CHAPTER SIX

"JUST NOW?" I ASKED.

"Yes."

"But that means someone's there. They're going to find his body."

"Right."

I'd never seen Nasty drop the ball or be ineffective. Never. In the years that I knew her, she'd demonstrated sound judgment and a level head in cases of extreme duress. But something about Gil's death had put her on edge.

"What are you going to do about it?"

Nasty raised her eyebrows. Until just then, I hadn't realized how far I thought she'd go.

"I'm going to go investigate, find Gil's body, and report it to the police. Big Bro will cooperate with their investigation."

"What are you going to tell Tex?"

"I don't answer to Tex." She paused, as if waiting for my response.

"I don't answer to Tex, either, if that's what you're implying."

"You're in a relationship with him. Call it what you want."

Nasty didn't show this side of herself often. To the rest of the world, she seemed to have her act together, juggling the demands of her two-year-old baby boy, her booming business, and her personal life. The baby was the son of a wealthy businessman with whom Nasty had indicated she was not receptive to a long-term commitment. Of every path available to her, she'd chosen the one with no resistance, the one that allowed her to live as she wanted to live and not answer to anyone—which, now that I thought about it, was a somewhat negative way to describe being in a relationship.

"Don't worry, Madison. I won't tell him you were there."

I got out of Nasty's Saab but kept my hand on the door while I stood there. Nasty had helped me out more than once, and now was the first time I felt I could return the favor. I reopened the door and bent down to address her.

"Do you remember my business manager, Effie?" I asked.

"Mid-twenties? Dated one of my employees a few years back?"

"Yes. She's good with computers. I can loan her out to you for a few days to help with your tech needs."

Nasty looked at me while she considered my suggestion. "You'll vouch for her?"

"For Effie? She's got that click-click-done millennial brain that understands technology in a way I don't. I brought her on as a part-timer to answer the phones and organize my calendar, and she set up an inventory system in the cloud and automated my banking. In her spare time, she's been studying mid-century modern classics so she can speak the language. She's a dream."

"Sounds good. Thanks. I'll meet you at your studio after I take care of this morning."

I stood back up and shut the door to Nasty's car. She was on her way before I'd made it to my side porch.

My house's side door was locked. I cupped my hands to my face and peered inside, but the door opened onto a solarium that led to the kitchen, so even if I had cleaned the windows recently, there wasn't much of a sightline in. I went around to the front door, which I rarely used, and tried it. Again, it was locked. When I looked through the glass of the door this time, I saw straight through from the Glenn Den to the living room to the kitchen.

I didn't see Lily, but I did see Rocky, who stood on the opposite side of the door and barked at me. He was overdue for a trim, and his long caramel and white fur was fluffed out around him, making him appear larger than he was. Something had him agitated. He turned around and went four steps in the other direction. Then he turned back to me, as if checking if I were following.

"I can't come in, Rock," I said. "I don't suppose you've learned how to unlock the door yet, have you?"

"Madison?" called Lily.

I turned away from my house and looked side to side.

Lily came around the corner. "Sorry about the locked doors. I didn't realize you don't have a spare set of keys."

I started to descend the stairs, and she came closer and held out my keychain.

"Here," she said.

I took the keys and unlocked the front door. Lily

followed me inside. Rocky ran forward and bounded around my ankles in greeting, and I scooped him up and ruffled his fur. Lily's behavior felt off, but I couldn't put my finger on what it was that bothered me. I carried Rocky to the kitchen, set him on the floor by his food bowl, then went to the solarium to get him a puppy treat. I glanced out the same window I'd peered into seconds before and realized what was off. The red Lexus was gone.

Lily was covering up that she'd had company. And after the morning she'd had, I was more than a little curious about who she'd called.

I pulled a doggie biscuit out of a treat bag and extended it to Rocky. He hopped up on his back paws and took it in his mouth then trotted away and left us alone. "There was a red Lexus parked out front. Was someone here?"

"That was Franklin Rich. He's the principal of Lakewood Prep School. I've been trying to arrange a meeting with him, since the boys are all going to be students there." She tucked her hair behind her ears. "The timing wasn't what I'd consider ideal, but I have to do what's best for the boys."

"I've never heard of a principal who makes house calls," I said, attempting to keep my voice light.

"We had a meeting set for this afternoon, but after what happened this morning, I didn't feel up to it. I called to reschedule, and he said he could pick up their transcripts in person."

"That was considerate."

Lily stood in the doorway, blocking my way into the kitchen. She stepped backward and let me through. Two yellow mugs sat on the table, one empty, one half-full. A ring of bright-pink lipstick that matched Lily's was on the empty one. I imagine if I invited my boy's new school principal to my house to hand over their school transcripts, I might have offered him a cup of coffee, so I dropped my suspicion and gave her the benefit of the doubt.

"I'm not sorry he's dead," she said quietly. She toyed with the fringes on a tea towel, not making eye contact with me. "For the past nine years, he's fought me on everything. He said as long as we were legally married, I couldn't see other men or I'd lose everything." She looked up. "Custody. He never wanted to be a father to my boys, but he threatened to take them from me to keep me in line."

"He can't threaten you anymore," I said.

"Do the police know?" she asked. "About Gil?"

"They will soon." I studied her. "I need to go to my studio and start working on the plan for your house. You should come with me. My office manager will be working off-site today, so you can use her desk to go through my inventory and mark anything you like."

For where to spend my workday, I had two options: the freestanding storage facility next to Thelma Johnson's house and the studio on Greenville Avenue where we now headed. I'd purchased the structure next to my house after a crash course in business expansion made it the obvious next decision for me, but I'd found it was a space best saved for after-hours projects, not client appointments. These days, the interior was a mess, filled with my parents' unpacked estate. I'd opened and closed two boxes, checking out the contents, before determining that I needed more time for that walk down memory lane.

Mad for Mod was my mid-century modern decorating business, and while I had a high percentage of return clients,

I also liked to be available for the occasional walk-in. The only people who walked through my neighborhood were the ones who lived in my development, and most of them had decorated their houses with mid-century modern furnishings the first time the style came around.

The drive to my studio was short, and I spent half of it trying to figure out what, if anything, I should say about the morning. Lily's behavior hadn't changed, but the lens through which I saw her had. I didn't know her well enough to give her the same blind loyalty I'd given others in similar situations, but she was Tex's family, and that meant a lot. I couldn't shake the anxious anticipation of the second shoe dropping. The longer it took for the police to learn of Gil's untimely death, the more questions I'd have to field from Tex. I had a twelve-year-old hooligan to thank for my reprieve; if Tex were on his A-game, he would have gotten all of the details out of me by now.

I parked in the lot behind my studio. Lily made no move to get out of the car, and I turned off the engine and sat with her. "Have you talked to your brother about this morning?" I asked.

"No," she said. "I called to check on the boys, and David told me what happened. I wanted to kill Gil the day he taught Gabe that laxative trick."

"You should probably stop saying that."

"What?" She stared at me for a few seconds before realizing what she'd said and why I told her not to say it again. "Oh." She turned away from me. "Oh." She turned back. "You don't think the police will suspect I had something to do with Gil's death, do you?'

"That's probably a question for Tex."

"Right." She toyed with a tassel that hung from her oversized brown and gold Louis Vuitton handbag.

"Listen, Lily, I don't want to come between you and Tex, but I don't feel right not telling him about this morning. Considering Gabe's prank, I think Tex will understand why I didn't say anything when I was at his condo, but the more time that passes, the worse it'll be."

"I love your relationship with my brother, and I can tell you know him better than most of the women he's dated. But trust me on this. Tex won't be mad about what we did. He'll be mad about what Gil did."

"What did Gil do?"

Lily pulled the envelope out of her bag and extended it to me. "See for yourself."

I opened the envelope and pulled out the signed divorce papers, only to discover they were neither signed nor divorce papers. They were pages of research about plants at the herbarium. The paper smelled faintly of ink. A running footer on the printed pages indicated the file name and date they'd been printed, which corresponded to today.

Gil had never intended to give Lily what she went to the arboretum to get, and if she wanted to kill him before she looked in that envelope, she'd only have more reason to want him dead now.

CHAPTER SEVEN

I FOLDED THE PAPERS AND THRUST THEM BACK INTO THE envelope, which I then extended to Lily. She dropped it back into the depths of her bag. Unlike my small wicker frame bag that held my wallet, keys, and emergency tube of SPF 90 sunscreen, hers was big enough to double as a carry-on. Those not-divorce-papers were as good as gone.

"I should feel bad," she said. "I should feel sad about Gil, but I don't. He made my life miserable because he could. He was up to something, and he got what he deserved. I don't think I should feel guilty about that." She looked up at me. "I didn't kill him, but I'm looking at the best possible scenario here. My divorce problems are over, and my boys won't have to grow up with a deadbeat as their father." She sighed. "But you're right. I need to tell my brother."

Satisfied that we were on the same page, I left the car and led her inside.

Mad for Mod was a typical storefront in a zoned district of businesses. The back entrance opened onto the hallway that led to the showroom. Even though I had a small lot out back, it was far more common for clients to park alongside the street out front and enter through the front door.

My office was on the right. The back wall of it was cork, covered in upholstery swatches, paint chips, and sample pages of new old stock tile. Every time I discovered a company stocking or sourcing mid-century materials, I added them to the wall so clients knew what we'd be working with.

For a long time, the office had housed a custom-built desk made for me by my handyman at the time and two Barcelona chairs on the opposite side of the desk for client consultations. Shortly after Effie joined my team, I'd added a second desk for her. Where mine was covered in swatch books, sketch pads, and colored pencils, hers had a keyboard, a mousepad, and a coaster for her coffee. Effie liked things just so.

Effie was at her desk. "Hey, boss," she said. Today she wore a yellow hoodie and matching sweatpants. Her hair was in a topknot. She stood from the desk and took Rocky from my arms. After cradling him against her chest, she set him down next to his water bowl. "I finished your billing and updated your software. And I finished the tagging project, but I wasn't sure if you wanted me to put the Sputnik lamps under classics or atomic or both." She glanced at Lily. "Is this Captain Allen's sister?"

Effie Jones was my one full-time employee. When we first met, she was a college student living in an apartment building that I secretly owned. Since then, she'd matured into a smart, capable woman with a business degree. The job market for smart, capable, recent college graduates with business degrees was saturated, though, and what had started out as a couple of hours here and there had turned into a full-time gig. While I thought of business in terms of MCM, Effie thought about it in terms of P&L, EBITDA, and GMROI. Considering the rest of her generation thought in terms of LOL and OMG, I was lucky to have found her.

Since coming on board, Effie had migrated my business practices from a paper calendar of appointments and a spreadsheet of inventory to databases for both. I now had my feet firmly planted in two different centuries: the one from which I drew inspiration and the one with the technology that matched my business growth. I suspected Effie liked working for me for more reasons than just the paycheck. Things weren't dull around my neck of the woods.

"Yes," I said. I formally introduced the two, trying to act like it was just another regular day at the office. I handed Rocky's leash over to Lily. "Can you take Rocky out for a short walk? I need to talk to Effie."

Lily nodded and took the leash. Rocky, who was always keen to make new friends, hopped around her ankles and then led her to the front door.

The chimes over the back door rang, and Nasty walked in. Nasty had changed her clothes since this morning. Now she wore a fitted white shirt tucked into low-rise black trousers, paired with black patent stiletto-heeled shoes, all of which put her four inches taller than me. You'd never know she'd dealt with a dead body mere hours ago. The woman was a marvel. Her long, copper-streaked hair was draped over her left shoulder, and a stray lock of hair swept her right cheekbone.

"Hey, Donna," Effie said. "How's Big Bro?"

"Did you tell her?" Nasty asked me.

"Tell me what?" Effie asked.

"I told Nas—" I caught myself— "I told Donna she could borrow you today."

Effie shifted her attention from me to Nasty. "I thought you had an automated 24-hour answering service to route your calls?"

"I don't want you to answer the phones. I need you on IT."

Effie froze. "You're going to give me access to your computer system?" she asked in hushed awe.

Nasty shrugged. "Madison says you're good with computers."

Effie looked at me, and I nodded. "We'll be fine here. Our next big job is going to be Lily's house in Midway Hills, so I'll set her up at your desk so she can cherry-pick the inventory between phone calls."

"Okay, Boss. If you say so." She zipped her small wallet-bag and then stepped out from behind the desk. Of the three of us, two knew about a certain incident this morning, and while two-thirds of us were acting like today was any other day, the third of us that wore my clothes was having a hard time functioning normally.

"Can I talk to you for a moment while Effie gets her things?" I asked Nasty.

"Sure."

I led Nasty to the front of my showroom and showed her an arrangement of coconut chairs by the front window. I moved a lot of furniture from my inventory based on my carefully curated displays, but this grouping had been passed over more than once. I pointed at a chair.

Nasty said, "I'll stand."

"They're very comfortable,"

"I'm sure they are. I'd rather stand."

"Fine." I sat in a coconut chair and looked up at Nasty. I wasn't pleased by the dynamic, so I stood. "What happened when you went back to the arboretum?"

"I placed a call to the police and told them about Gil. I waited until two detectives arrived. I showed them the silent alarm and explained that Gil had a habit of tripping it."

I paced back and forth a few steps. "But who tripped the alarm the second time?"

"I wouldn't sweat it," Nasty said. "It's possible the person who killed Gil came back to cover up evidence. Or maybe he or she didn't have to come back. Maybe the killer was hiding in the arboretum while we were there."

The thought sent a chill through me. Everything Nasty said was true—or, if not true, then possible. The only thing I knew for certain was that Gil Banks was dead when I got there, and that alone removed suspicion from Lily.

CHAPTER EIGHT

After Nasty and Effie left, I gave Lily a crash course in searching my inventory and left her alone while I went to the showroom.

Lily and I spent the rest of the working day discussing design concepts and going through the inventory for her new house. It was my favorite sort of project: a long-ignored property had more potential than one that had been updated with modern touches. Dallas used to be filled with mid-century ranches ripe for my decorating skills, but the housing market had lent itself toward flippers who bought low, gutted everything I loved about the properties, and replaced those era-specific details with generic materials purchased with a corporate discount from a wholesale store. New home buyers didn't particularly love paying me a commission to undo a renovation that was less than a year old, so my business model shifted more to design than renovation.

This ranch was different.

Sometime after discussing color palettes ("masculine enough for the boys but something for me too," which I interpreted as "green"), I set Lily up with my big book of design ideas, which Effie had compiled from various water- and mold-damaged back issues of magazines I'd acquired through estate purchases the past few years. I also handed Lily a packet of sticky notes. "Tag the pages of rooms you like. I'm going to take Rocky out for a quick bathroom break."

I clipped on Rocky's leash, and we went out the front door. I waved to the owner of the Salvadorean Restaurant across the street and then gave Rocky the lead. He led me to the corner, where he peed on a telephone pole.

A dark grey sedan parked alongside the curb out front. Two people got out of the car, one middle-aged with a paunch around her midsection, the other a Mexican man in an athletic-cut suit. I recognized the woman. She was Sue Niedermeier, one of Tex's most revered homicide detectives. The man was a stranger.

"Hi, Madison," Sue called out.

One of the unique benefits of dating the local police captain was being on a first-name basis with his staff. I'd come to know Sue over the course of a couple of cases and found her and her regular partner effective at their jobs but as human as the rest of us.

"Hi, Sue," I said. "Where's Ling?"

"She had the nerve to take a vacation," Sue said. "Can you believe it? She went to the Rock and Roll Hall of Fame. They gave me Andy Samberg here to pick up the slack."

"Is he any good?"

"He thinks *Brooklyn Nine-Nine* was a documentary series."

"I resent that," the younger detective said.

"Just kidding. Jerry's okay." She turned to him. "Jerry, this is Madison Night. Madison, this is Detective Jerry Jones."

I raised my eyebrows.

"My parents are Cowboys fans," he said. "My mom was pregnant with me the year Jerry Jones bought the team."

"He's thirty-three," Sue said with a roll of her eyes. "A baby."

Jerry looked suitably embarrassed by his age.

Despite the friendly atmosphere, I knew the presence of two homicide detectives meant this wasn't a social call. "If you're looking for Captain Allen, he's not here," I said, hoping that assumption seemed plausible on my part.

"We're looking for Ms. Lily Banks," Jerry said. "We heard she was here."

"Lily?—she—"

"Hi, officers." Lily stood in the doorway of Mad for Mod, the picture of calm. She smiled broadly, as if welcoming the detectives to a housewarming party.

"I'm Lily Allen. Banks is my married name, but I've been separated for close to a decade, and I go by my maiden name."

"Ms. Allen," Sue said. She looked at Jerry and then at Lily again. "Is there some place we can talk in private?"

"Use my office," I said.

"Madison's practically family," Lily said at the same time. "You can talk freely in front of her." She dropped into one of the coconut chairs and looked up at the three of us. As if on cue, Rocky ran into the showroom and hopped up on Lily's lap. She stroked his fur while he turned in a circle and then flopped across her thighs. Who could suspect the person holding the Shih Tzu? Nice going, Lil.

"Ms. Banks," Jerry said.

"Allen," Lily corrected.

Jerry looked at Sue, who nodded. Jerry continued. "Ms. Allen, we have some bad news. Your husband's body was found this morning."

Lily stopped stroking Rocky's fur, and he lifted his head and looked at her. Then he rested back on his furry paws.

"He's my husband in legal terms only," Lily said quietly. "I came to Dallas to finalize our divorce."

None of it was a lie, but the way she phrased that seemed too careful to have been accidental. What was she playing at?

"When was the last time you spoke to him?" Sue asked.

"Yesterday." Lily took in Sue and Jerry's faces. "He gave me the keys to his house. It was part of the divorce settlement."

"Where is this house?"

Lily looked at me.

"Midway Hills," I supplied.

"Madison was with me when I met with Gil," Lily said. "It wasn't a friendly encounter." She glanced up at me as if giving me permission to agree. I nodded because her words were true. Everything she said was true. Lily knew how to handle herself around these detectives. They were here to do a job, and she seemed to recognize that. I admired her level head.

Sue turned to me unexpectedly. "What happened?"

"Gil gave Lily the address to a house he described as move-in ready. He showed up, gave her the keys, and left. We went inside and found the condition to be pretty much anything but."

"Did you confront him about it?" Jerry asked Lily.

"I called him about it, if that's what you mean. He said he'd hired a company to stage the house for me after he moved out but didn't have time to go through it himself to check their work. It was classic Gil to blame it on someone else."

"Did he say why he moved out?"

"He got a job in New Zealand," Lily said. "I don't know the details, but it must have been lucrative, because after nine years of ignoring my requests for a divorce, he changed his mind and agreed to everything I wanted."

"Do you know any details about this new job?"

Lily shook her head. "He's a botanist. He and his partner conducted research at the Lakewood Arboretum."

"What's this partner's name?" Jerry asked.

"Ed Bishop."

Jerry and Sue exchanged glances. I shifted my attention to Lily, who'd started petting Rocky again. She hadn't said anything about Gil's business partner until now, and that seemed like either an odd omission or a convenient fact.

"Did Ed work at the arboretum with Gil?" I asked.

All eyes turned to me.

"Sorry," I quickly added. I held up both hands. "I'm not the one who should be asking questions."

Sue looked at Jerry and then back at me. "We haven't been able to reach Mr. Bishop. The arboretum general manager was at the lab when we arrived. He told us there were signs of a break-in."

"Was anything stolen?" I asked.

"Some research was deleted from Mr. Banks's computer," Sue said. "The buffer in the printer indicated it had been printed recently, but we didn't find anything to match."

"How did he die?" Lily asked.

"The preliminary findings indicate he ingested a poisonous plant toxin, which, as a botanist, he would have known not to eat."

"That sounds like a bad way to die," I said.

"When you find a good way to die, let me know," Sue said.

"It also sounds like his murder had something to do with his work at the lab," I added.

"It's one of the angles we're considering," Jerry said.

"Sorry, Madison," Sue said. "You know we can't tell you anything else."

The statement seemed obvious, but it also felt as if I were leading them down a path away from Lily. All I could think about was the sheaf of freshly printed pages that Lily had in her handbag, the envelope of research that she'd thought was divorce papers that she'd taken from the lab that morning when we found Gil's body. Someone had set her up.

Sue pulled a business card from her jacket pocket and handed it to Lily. "If you think of anything that could help us with our investigation, let me know."

"I'm sorry," Lily said, ignoring the card. "Gil and I have been living separate lives for almost a decade. I don't know anything about his life here in Dallas."

"What about the boys?" I asked without thinking. I was so used to being on the side of the police that it hadn't occurred to me to keep my questions to myself. As soon as this one was out of my mouth, I regretted it.

Again, all eyes turned to me.

"Did they ever come visit their father?" I elaborated.

"Last month," Lily said. "The boys play baseball, and when we learned we were moving here, I asked Gil to arrange an introduction to the local coach. George came up for the weekend and stayed with him."

"How many sons do you have?" Sue asked.

"Four. My oldest, David, is in high school. He was in Houston on a college recruiting trip."

"How old are your sons?"

"Adam is ten, and Gabe is twelve. Gil left before Adam turned one. He and Gabe don't have a clear memory of their father."

"What about George and David?"

"George is fifteen, and David is seventeen. I knew they needed a male presence in their lives, so I got them started in Little League early. Baseball became the only sport our family cared about." Lily looked at Jerry. "No offense."

Jerry shrugged. "I'm a hockey guy myself."

"Gil was good with the boys," Lily continued. "It was his one redeeming quality. When David turned ten, Gil took him on camping trips and taught him about nature."

"What about George?"

Lily shook her head. "George never forgave Gil for leaving. I'm not sure he forgave me for not getting him back."

CHAPTER NINE

UNTIL LILY SAID IT, I'D NEVER STOPPED TO THINK ABOUT WHAT growing up without a father had been like for her boys. Tex didn't talk about them other than to say he looked out for Lily when they were growing up, and I remembered something about him not liking Gil and her not liking Tex having an opinion about her taste in men. It was classic sibling behavior. With Tex and Lily's parents out of the picture early, Tex had rebelled against societal norms, and Lily had rebelled against Tex.

I didn't believe for one second that Tex had neglected to keep tabs on the boys, even if Lily didn't want him to. He had a natural tendency to protect people, which manifested in his choice of career. I'd missed the bad-boy years of his life and met him around the tail end of his bachelor days, but his familiarity with the dancers at Jumbo's, the local strip club, and his failed relationship with Nasty both spoke of the version of Tex from which mine had evolved.

Personal growth was a wonderful thing.

Sue and Jerry offered condolences for Lily's loss and said goodbye. Sue lingered behind while Jerry went out the front door. She called me over to her.

"Is everything okay with Captain Allen?" she asked. "I gave him a courtesy call when we heard about the connection between his sister and the victim. He didn't answer, and he hasn't returned any of my messages."

"He had a bout of food poisoning," I said, which felt close enough to the truth. But because I knew Sue well, I added, "The last time I saw him, he wasn't able to travel far from the bathroom."

She laughed. "Been there, done that." She pointed past me. "You'll let me know if you learn anything relevant, right?"

"Of course," I said, though I had a childish urge to cross my fingers behind my back when I said it.

I waited until the detectives' car pulled away from the curb before I headed back into my studio. I found Lily in my office.

"That went well," Lily said.

"Did it?"

"They know about the murder, and they're investigating it."

I sat in one of the Barcelona chairs opposite my desk. "How did they know you were here?"

"It's not a secret, is it? I left a message with David so they could find me if they needed me."

"Did you talk to Tex?"

"I called him first, but he didn't answer."

I'd accepted Tex not talking to Sue as behavior driven by his morning's inconvenience, but not answering when Lily called didn't feel right. I checked my phone for messages and, seeing none, called him. The call went to voicemail. I hung up and shook my head.

When I needed to clear my mind, I found the best thing to do was work. A few weeks ago, I noticed a construction crew at a house that I passed on my way into the studio. A quick chat with one of the workers revealed the house was being flipped by a husband-wife team who'd recently gotten into the business. I showed up the next day with a tray of coffee, a smile, and a proposal, and I walked away with a handshake agreement to get first dibs on anything the crew tore out of the existing structure. The resulting haul was a Universal range with a built-in portable James dishwasher—something of a unicorn in terms of mid-century modern appliances. Universal stoves were somewhat popular in the fifties, but this pu-pu platter of kitchen needs in one fixture never fully caught the public's attention. My electrician was quick to point out the faulty wiring and strongly recommended I use the piece for nothing that required electricity. I offered him a bonus if he could bring it up to code. He changed his tune pretty quickly after that. Severe rust damage to the paint job was the only lasting problem, which I solved with a trip to the powder coater.

I'd also acquired a set of blue bathroom fixtures and a code-compliant spiral staircase made of steel. The last one was similar to the staircase in Rock Hudson's apartment in *Pillow Talk*, and I was so excited about the prospect of using it in a design that I hadn't been able to sleep that night.

I cleared my current street-facing windows to make room for the Universal range, which was due to be delivered today. Modern technology had made it so old ovens were at the bottom of most homeowner's wish lists, which freed me up to go with a novelty design. I'd had the powder coaters use Tiger 149/33670, a sweet pink shade somewhere between strawberry meringue cookies and pink Peeps. There was no particular demand for pink kitchen appliances, but the color made me happy.

In preparation for my new windows, I'd asked Effie to go through my stash of Pyrex and pull out anything pink. A cart now sat in the showroom, stacked with mixing bowls and covered casserole dishes. The pièce de résistance was a set of solid pink mixing bowls, not because they were any rarer than the other pieces in my collection but because they'd been stored, unused, in their original box. A similar set was listed on Etsy for over two thousand dollars!

I'd taken the smallest of a collection of Pyrex bowls with me to my local paint store and requested the owner match the color, then painted the temporary wall at the back of the window with it, accented with hand-drawn daisies that mimicked the pattern on the Pyrex. I found two cartons of white milk glass vases in the back of my inventory and filled them with paper daisies, then positioned them along the top of the cabinets. A row of cannisters labeled Flour, Sugar, Tea, and Coffee lined the countertop, and a hodgepodge of colorful mugs hung from small gold hooks that I'd screwed into the bottom of the cabinets. The result said "Springtime" in a way a temporary Easter bunny would not.

Effie, who'd gotten pretty good at reading my mind, had added a pink hand mixer and a stack of vintage tea towels in various atomic patterns. The only other thing I'd need to make my vision a reality was a fake kitchen counter, which I'd assigned to my newest employee, a high school senior with a gift for woodworking. The requested prop was already installed.

Before Lily's scheduled arrival in Dallas, I'd emptied out my display window and hung a black curtain across the front. The curtain signaled to the neighborhood and passing traffic that they would soon see a new display, which tended to raise people's interest. I'd had every intention of getting the kitchen display in place before opening today so I could capitalize on traffic passing by, but today hadn't gone as planned. I also didn't know what time the appliances were slated to arrive. I went back to my office, where Lily was flipping through a swatch book of carpet samples. There, I untacked the powder coater's business card from my wall of cork and called him.

"Barrera Coatings," answered a gravelly voice. A fit of coughing followed shortly.

"This is Madison Night. I was expecting a delivery of —"

"The pink stuff, right? Yeah, we had to get that out of our showroom. Not what our customers expect to see when they walk in, know what I mean?"

In circles that had nothing to do with mid-century modern interior design, Barrera Powder Coating was known for their slick, colorful treatment of hot rods and motorcycles. I never really considered what a set of pink kitchen appliances might say to prospective customers other than "our clients have really excellent taste," but perhaps I was biased.

"Then the truck is on its way?"

"Truck's already back."

"I'm at my showroom, and if there's a delivery of pink kitchen appliances here, it's news to me."

"Hold on." The man put me on hold. He came back in under a minute. "Your showroom is on Monticello, right?"

"No, it's on Greenville."

"Hold on." The line went quiet for a few seconds and then switched over to music.

While I waited, Lily held up a swatch book. "What do you think of this one?" she asked.

I leaned forward. Her finger was on a square of navy blue Berber carpeting.

"It's not the most exciting swatch in the book," I said.

"I have four boys. Berber is indestructible, right?"

"Do you want your new home life to be grounded by navy blue construction-grade carpeting?" I asked. The music on the other end of the phone stopped, and I held up my index finger to Lily to hold her thought.

"Hello?" I asked.

"Yeah, there's a note here. We delivered to the address on file in the M streets."

"There wasn't anybody at that address this morning. Did your team just leave the delivery out front?"

"No. Says here it was signed for by J. Nussbaum. Is that one of your employees?"

"Yes, but—"

"I've got a line out my front door. Check with your employee and call me back if there's a problem with the paint job." A click sounded in my ear.

"Is everything okay?" Lily asked.

"I don't know." I checked the clock. The afternoon had already come, but Jimmy Nussbaum, my part-time, seventeen-year-old handyman, wasn't scheduled to arrive until after eighth period let out. "Get your things. We're closing early to handle a fixture emergency at my other studio."

Lily closed the swatch book on the desk. "It's just as well. I'm too distracted to make any solid decisions."

While I was tempted to use the drive to Thelma Johnson's house to ask questions about Gil's business, I knew my more important role was distraction, so I played to my strengths and shared my theory on design.

"I believe everybody has something, some décor object, that they love. It could be that it holds a special meaning, or it reminds the owner of a vacation, or maybe it was a family heirloom. Once I discover that item, I can design an entire room around it."

"What about a whole house?"

"There's a first time for everything," I said, smiling. "When we get to my place, maybe you can go through the contents of the moving truck and pull out a few of your and the boys' favorite things. That will give me a jumping-off point."

"The boys are easy. David likes *Star Trek* and George likes girls. Adam and Gabe like baseball."

"What about you? What do you like?"

"Wine." She laughed. "Honestly, it's been so long since I thought about what I wanted that I don't know where to start. I guess that's finally going to change."

A few minutes later, we turned the corner to Monticello. The moving truck was still parked out along the side hedges. I turned the corner so I could park in front of my satellite office and found a white delivery van already sitting there. Two men dressed in neon yellow T-shirts and baggy jeans stood by the back of the van. I'd been under the impression that the fixtures had already been delivered and that Jimmy had instructed the service to unload them inside, but my signals appeared to have gotten crossed.

I parked, and we got out of the car. One of the men stepped away from the truck and blocked our path.

"Lily Banks?" he asked. He stared at me for an uncomfortable stretch and then at Lily.

"Madison Night," I said. I held out my hand, although the man's demeanor did not suggest this was an impromptu business meeting. "I'm the business owner. If you have a delivery, it's for me."

The men looked at each other. The second man, lankier than the first, shrugged.

The first man turned back to us. "Sure, we got a delivery. A delivery for Lily Banks."

"It's Allen, not Banks," Lily said, stepping forward. She held Rocky closely. Her bold move surprised me—I would have expected her to be more timid, less confrontational.

The men exchanged a look again, and this time the larger one smirked. "Call yourself whatever you want, lady, but the name on the invoice says Banks." He walked around to the back of the van.

My heart thumped in my chest. It was broad daylight, but the street was empty, my neighbors either at work or busy doing crosswords. I stepped closer to Lily, not because I felt a fifty-something woman in a vintage blue A-line dress with patch pockets and Keds lent any menace to the situation, but because I didn't want her to feel alone.

The stout man held out a clipboard. "You wanna sign or should I put down an *X*?"

Lily said, "You can do whatever you want. I've never been

involved in my ex-husband's business, and I don't plan to get involved now." She handed Rocky to me and pulled out her phone. "I'm calling the police. Did I mention my brother is the captain?"

"Yeah, but he's not here, is he?" the lanky man said.

The stout man drew a large X on his clipboard and tore off the top sheet. He nodded at the lanky man, who grabbed the handles on the van's back doors. With a jerky motion, he unlatched the doors and stepped back as they opened, dumping a mountain of dry brown dirt onto the hood of my car.

CHAPTER TEN

"WHAT ARE YOU DOING?" I CRIED, TOO LATE. A PILE OF LOOSE dirt poured out of the van, as if it had been packed against the doors just to ensure this dramatic display.

If I hadn't been holding Rocky, I would have run forward and pushed the lanky man out of the way. But loose dirt floated through the air, getting in Rocky's eyes. He blinked a few times and shook his head, hitting me in the face with his long fur. He squirmed with discomfort, and I held him close to comfort him.

My anger was reflected with mild amusement, confirming that these men didn't see me or my killer Shih Tzu as a threat. The lanky man shook the dirt off the hem of his pants. He raised his finger and pointed at me and then Lily.

"There's more dirt where that comes from. Your husband might be out of the picture, but now it's your turn to step up." He crumbled up the piece of paper in his hand, tossed it on top of the dirt pile, then slapped his partner's arm. "Let's get out of here."

The men climbed into their van and pulled away, leaving behind enough dirt to fill a grave.

The city of Dallas swept the major thoroughfares once a month, but the curb in front of residential properties was the homeowners' responsibility. I'd fought and lost the battle against citations more than once, learning to either factor street cleaning into my daily work or pad my budgets to cover penalties. But this, a mountain of dirt dumped on the side of the street outside of my satellite office, wasn't the same as a pile of empty paint cans. I couldn't vacuum this up with the ShopVac. The breeze caught hold of the top layer of dirt and scattered it farther into the street.

Lily stared at the dirt. Her face had lost all color. She seemed rooted to the sidewalk, unable to move. I stepped closer to the dirty pile, plucked the balled-up invoice from the top, then smoothed it out. The top of the paper said Lakewood Arboretum, and across the notes part, someone had written "dirt delivery."

On top of the expected city citation for this much dirt, I would have to wash my car, but neither issue was as important as Lily. I shook my foot free from dirt, feeling some of it enter my sneaker, and turned to her. "Let's go inside."

Lily nodded. With my guidance, she turned around and walked toward my satellite office. I unlocked the doors, and she entered ahead of me. I set Rocky on the concrete floor, and he took off for his bed. Cartons sat just inside the door, as I'd hoped, but even those would have to wait for later.

I filled two pink Blendo glasses with water from the

cooler, handed one to Lily, then led her to the front of my showroom, where four Wassily chairs were positioned around a glass and chrome coffee table. Two thick binders filled with color photos of rooms I'd designed sat on the chairs, available for clients to peruse. I moved both binders to the table and sat, gesturing for Lily to join me.

She did.

"Do you know those men?"

Lily shook her head. "I don't know anything about Gil's business. As far as I knew, he was a botanist conducting private research at the local arboretum."

"He never mentioned anything about his work?"

"Gil and I could barely be in the same room together, and when we were, our conversation was a little more targeted than small talk about our jobs."

"Did you ever threaten him in public?"

She looked up. "All the time."

"Witnesses?"

"Our fights were legendary. Somewhere out there, a Spaghetti Warehouse waitress is still talking about the time I dumped a plate of meatballs into his lap." She stifled a grin. "He had a meeting with some financiers that afternoon and couldn't go home to change."

As Lily temporarily lost herself in the memory of humiliating her now-deceased ex-husband, I considered more troubling facts. Someone had connected Lily to Gil. Someone wanted something that Gil was no longer around to give, and they appeared to have turned their attention to Lily.

"You need to tell Tex about those guys. The police will agree that was a threat. It'll only help you to have them on your side now and not have to wade through this stuff later."

Lily pulled her phone out and made a call. When someone answered, she said, "David, it's Mom. Can you put your uncle on the phone?" She paused. "Why not?" Pause. She stood and turned her back to me. "When?"

I stood too. "What happened?" I asked.

She held up her index finger. "I'll be there as soon as I can." She hung up and turned to me. "He's at the ER." Then she grabbed her handbag.

"Dehydration because of the laxative?"

"Bee sting. *Stings.*"

"Tex is allergic to bee stings?"

"Severely. You didn't know?"

I shook my head. "He never mentioned it."

I put up a baby fence to keep Rocky from running loose around broken fixtures and we left.

We reached my car. The dirt had settled around the wheels. Lily pulled the keys to her moving van out of her handbag. "I'll drive the van."

While she drove, Lily filled me in on the details of Tex's allergy. "The first time he got stung, his throat almost swelled shut. He was ten. Our mom was out. He didn't tell anybody, just went to his room and drank about a gallon of water, hoping it would pass. When Bo saw him, he took Tex to the emergency room."

"Bo was your older brother?"

"Yes." She shook her head. "When my mom found out what happened, she went nuts."

"I imagine that's the sort of thing that most mothers would go nuts over."

"No, she wasn't worried about Tex. She was mad Bo took him to the emergency room. She said her insurance rates would go up. She grounded all three of us."

Tex had told me very little about his mother. When he had, it wasn't during the best of times for him, but it was the first time he opened up to me and let me see more than the protector role he played for everyone else. Those early moments of sharing stories about our lives were the most intimate we'd been up to that point, and even though I hadn't been ready for it at the time, I could look back and see that was the beginning of something more than I'd expected to come from our relationship.

Lily and I arrived at the hospital. The sun was descending, and a pinkish salmon hue colored the sky. Swatches of clouds, like broad strokes from a paintbrush, mottled the shade, dulling down the vibrance. David was waiting for us in the parking lot.

"Hey, Mom," he said nervously. He glanced quickly at me. "It happened really fast. I called 9-1-1, and they sent an ambulance. I told George to take Gabe and Adam back to Uncle Tex's house and stay inside. Is he going to be okay?"

"You did good," Lily said. "Wait here. We're going to talk to the doctors and find out his condition."

Visiting Tex in the hospital wasn't a unique experience. People liked to shoot at cops, and more than once, Tex had caught a bullet. In a recent case, we'd gone so far as to release a statement that he'd died because of gunfire to trick the shooter into revealing themselves. It's amazing what you'll agree to do in the name of love.

Being the family and romantic partner of the police captain got you a certain number of benefits, and at the hospital, we were ushered past the waiting room to a temporary hospital bed. The intern pulled back a curtain, and at first glance, I was certain we'd been led to the wrong patient. Tex's face was puffy. The eye that wasn't discolored from the baseball bat swing was swollen shut. His overall coloring was red. He wore a hospital gown, and his arms were dotted with small red puncture wounds surrounded by paler halos, each surrounded by a shaggy rash. At least fourteen stings covered his arms.

"Thup," he said in greeting.

"What happened?" Lily asked.

"Got thung."

Despite Tex's obvious discomfort, it was hard not to smile. The Greenwood Cemetery was a short walk from Tex's townhouse, and it was on a walk through there that I'd gotten an insight into who he was under the many layers of bro. He'd taken me to the grave of his grandfather, a Union soldier in the middle of a sea of Confederates. Brother fighting brother, Tex had said. The memory reminded me of what family meant to him.

The curtain pulled aside, and a nurse came into the already-tight space. She pulled the curtain closed behind her. "Hopefully all that charm you saved up when you came in is being used on these two, because you sure didn't use it on any of us."

"Theth two didn't thoot me full of antihithaminth with a thix-inth-long needle."

"That injection is the difference between you getting out of here and you lying unconscious in a cemetery." She turned to us. "I would love to hear Captain Allen explain what happened this morning, but in the interest of saving time, I'll tell you what I know."

Tex scowled.

"We got a call from"—she checked her clipboard—"David Banks. He said a swarm of bees had descended on his uncle in Greenwood Cemetery and that after being stung multiple times, he collapsed. Passing out isn't a common side effect of bee stings, so we checked his charts and discovered he was allergic. We sent out an ambulance and brought him here for treatment." She glanced at him. "He was dehydrated, which made his condition worse."

"How are you treating him?" I asked her.

"Things were going the wrong direction when he came in, so we administered an antihistamine and an anti-inflammatory to counter the stings, plus a beta agonist to relieve his breathing symptoms. Other than that, we're replenishing his fluids through an IV and assigning him bed rest."

"For how long?" Tex asked.

She shrugged. "Twenty-four hours to start with. Maybe more. We have a team of interns coming through this afternoon, and you'd make a great case for their observation."

Tex turned away from us and crossed his arms. "Thon of a bith."

I wasn't the sort of person to laugh at someone else's pain, but in Tex's case, it was hard not to. Even Tex seemed to recognize it.

"Thorry, Lil. I'm thuppothed to be helping you move to Dallath. I never expected thith to happen."

"Don't sweat it," Lily said. She glanced at me. "Madison's been a huge help already."

Tex looked back and forth between us. He appeared to detect something he didn't trust in the energy Lily and I shared, and his eyebrows dropped down low over his eyes. With his already discolored eye socket and swollen face, he was starting to look like a monster out of Rick Baker's special effect studio.

"Lily, we need to tell him," I said.

"Tell me what?" Tex turned his attention to Lily. "Whatth going on?"

Lily remained silent. "If you won't, I will," I added. It was less a threat than a gentle nudge in case she found speaking the words too difficult.

She held up her hand to me as if to indicate it wasn't necessary for me to step in. "It's okay, Madison." She took a deep breath, and her chest rose and then fell. "Gil's dead," she said. "He died this morning."

The swelling and discoloration in several of Tex's facial features made his response hard to describe, but he never looked away from Lily's face.

She didn't offer any other words, and I fought against filling the silence with my own. Tex still didn't look at me. He kept his eyes trained on his sister. Whatever silent communication passed between them, it was part of the Allen gene code, and I didn't know how to break it.

"Have you told the boyth?"

"Not yet. Where are they?"

"David rode in the ambulanth with me. He left George in charge of Gabe and Adam."

David had already told us as much. I glanced at Lily, who

had more than any one person could be expected to handle on her plate.

For the first time of the day, Lily appeared tired. Her face was pale, more cement than peaches and cream, and circles had appeared underneath her eyes. "I have to talk to David," she said. She turned around and left.

Before I could jump in and tell Tex anything else about the morning—and a lot was building up behind that dam—a woman in terracotta-colored scrubs pulled the curtain aside. She pushed a cart into the room. A syringe sat in an aluminum tray next to a few packets of alcohol-drenched wipes and a pair of blue rubber gloves.

"Hi, Captain," she said. "Good news. We found a bed for you in the ICU."

"Not thaying."

"That's not up to you," she said. She tore open an alcohol pad and wiped his arm. "Just lay back and relax. It's time for your next shot." She prepped the syringe and injected the contents into Tex's arm.

I stood back and waited for the process to be completed. My bad knee was starting to throb, so I glanced around for an empty chair. That was when I spotted Lily's handbag. She'd left so suddenly she must have forgotten it.

I picked it up and held it on my lap while the nurse finished with Tex. His eyes were at half-mast. He turned to me and held out his hand.

"What do you want?" I asked.

"You," he said.

I slipped my hand into his, and he ran his thumb over my fingers a few times.

"Watch out for Lily while I'm in here," he said. "Thee'th

not tough like you." He closed his eyes, fighting for a moment to stay awake but losing the battle.

The intern tossed the disposable supplies in the hazardous waste bin. "You can stay if you'd like, but it won't be much of a visit. He's probably going to sleep for the next few hours."

I inquired about the location of the waiting room, and then I stood. Lily's bag fell to the floor, landing on its side and spilling its contents. The sheaf of papers Gil had passed off as divorce papers fell out. Something about them seemed curious, especially now that I knew about the deleted research at Gil's lab. I didn't think it was a violation of her privacy to look at them a second time, so I unfolded the pages and smoothed them out, surprised to find they weren't the notes we'd taken from the arboretum at all. They were school transcripts, one for each of the boys. Lily had told me she gave these to the principal of the school system when he was at my house earlier today, but if that was the truth, then why was she still carrying them in her handbag?

CHAPTER ELEVEN

MY BAD KNEE DIDN'T MAKE SQUATTING EASY, BUT I WASN'T keen on sitting on the hospital room floor, so I corralled the rest of the spilled contents back inside the handbag and stood. Tex was fast asleep in his bed. I was about to reach back into Lily's bag for the envelope with the printed notes when David walked in.

"Hey," he said. "My mom asked me to come see if you were ready to leave."

I shoved the transcripts back into Lily's bag and hoisted it onto my shoulder. "Sure." I reached out for Tex's hand and squeezed it. Then I bent down and whispered, "Don't worry about your sister," I whispered. "I'll look out for her." I brushed his dark blond hair away from his swollen face, kissed his forehead, then followed David out of the room.

It was a crowded ride away from the hospital, with David, Lily, and me all packed into the front of the moving truck. I didn't know if Tex had heard my promise or not, but I felt somehow responsible for Lily and the boys while he was down for the count.

I also didn't know if Lily had told David about Gil's murder. Regardless of how Lily felt about her husband, Gil was the father of her sons, and they may have had an entirely different relationship with him than she did. There wasn't much I felt comfortable saying on the drive, so I kept my mouth shut while Lily drove me home. She eased the moving truck behind my dirty Alfa Romeo and turned to David.

"Wait here," she said. "I need to talk to Madison alone for a moment."

"Sure, Mom."

Lily climbed out of her side, and I climbed down from mine. She met me on the sidewalk. "Did you tell my brother about the men and the dirt?"

"No."

"Thank you," she said.

Before she could conclude that I was willing to keep secrets from Tex, I added, "I might have, but his schedule for drugs interrupted our conversation." I turned to her. "Why didn't you tell him the truth when you had the chance?"

"I was going to. I was. But you have to understand something. My brother's taken care of me since I was ten. And when I was ten, that was great. But do you know what it's like to have someone hovering over you and challenging your decisions when you're in your forties?"

I shook my head. What she described didn't sound all that bad, but my reaction was probably informed by my own sense of loss from decades ago. "I didn't have any siblings," I said.

"I sound ungrateful. I'm not. I love my brother. I wouldn't

be moving to Dallas if I didn't. But I wanted to do this—at least some of it—on my own."

"Which part?"

"The divorce. The move. Getting the boys set up at their schools. All of it. But does it matter? Even if I wanted my brother's help, he's not available."

"He'll recover. Besides, maybe it's all for the best. Maybe he'll come out of this with a little more sympathy for what life is like for you."

Lily let herself grin. "I never thought of that."

Between Gil's murder and Tex's hospitalization, Lily and I had been on a roller coaster ride since this morning. It was well past workday hours, and even if I'd had a regular workday, Mad for Mod would be closed by now. Twenty-four hours ago, the plan had been for Lily and the boys to move into the house in Midway Hills, for Gil to hand over the signed divorce papers and move on to his international botanist opportunity, for Tex to have the boys over for steaks, and for me to pop in as the charming, notorious, Doris Day-loving girlfriend-slash-decorator meeting her boyfriend's sister and kids for the first time. I barely knew how to pivot through this number of twists.

"I should be getting back to my boys," Lily said. "I need to tell them what happened."

"Would you like company? For moral support?"

"No. I need to handle this on my own."

"Are you going to be okay at Tex's?"

"I'm sure my brother has a pair of police department sweats for me to sleep in."

"Top left drawer of his dresser," I said, smiling. I removed a key from my keychain and handed it to her. "You have my number. Call me if you need anything. Tex keeps the spare keys to his Jeep in the cookie jar on the kitchen counter. If you want company, I'll be there in fifteen minutes. If I don't hear from you tonight, I'll see you at Mad for Mod tomorrow. Okay?"

Lily took the key and stared at it. "There is one thing you can do," she said.

"Name it."

"I'm supposed to meet with the school principal later this week. Gil was going to be there. Now, after everything that happened today—I don't—I'd rather avoid questions. Do you think—I don't even know how to ask."

And because I promised Tex I'd look out for his sister while he was indisposed, I said the first thing that came to mind. "I'll handle it." I didn't know exactly when I would fit that meeting into my schedule, but it was the least I could do.

*　*　*

LILY WAITED by the curb until I entered my house. For as long as I'd owned the property, I'd thought of it as Thelma Johnson's, but tonight, it was mine. It didn't matter how I'd come to have my name on the deed. Something had shifted, and the previously temporary feeling of ownership seemed permanent. If we'd been balancing on tectonic plates all day, Thelma Johnson's property was solid ground.

I collected Rocky from the office, and he relieved himself on the corner of the garden and then climbed up the concrete stairs, his fluffy overgrown fur dragging against the concrete. He entered the house when I opened the door. I dropped my keys on a small green and yellow vintage mosaic tile plate that wasn't appropriately sized for much else. I was fifty shades of dirty, but there was something more pressing than a shower in my immediate future.

People often thought that because I decorated in mid-century modern style using authentic fixtures and materials, I didn't rely on modern technology for conducting business. That assumption was the most foolish I'd encountered, and in more than one instance, being underestimated worked in my favor. I opened my laptop and navigated to the Lakewood Arboretum then to the Staff page, scrolled past the board of directors and general manager, and found what I wanted: botanists in residence. Professional headshots of Gil Banks and his research partner, Ed Bishop, sat to the left of individual bios. Gil's picture showed a younger version of himself: more hair, less belly, teeth pre-bleaching. His partner was completely bald, with a fluffy gray mustache. Having never met him, I didn't know how closely this photo resembled him, but I couldn't really see how much he might have changed. The page listed a direct number. I picked up my cell phone, and a message greeted me: "You've reached Bishop & Banks Research at the Lakewood Arboretum. Leave a message." I hung up.

I didn't expect to learn anything new about Gil from the public-facing portion of the arboretum website, especially since both Gil and Ed were akin to freelancers temporarily using the property, but I'd been hoping for contact information. Earlier today, when the detectives came to my studio, Sue had indicated that they hadn't been able to reach Ed.

I couldn't help but wonder if that was suspect. Someone had murdered Gil with a toxic plant. One would think a botanist would know not to ingest poisonous plant matter, but one might also think a botanist would know how to disguise a deadly plant in the first place.

I called the number again and this time left a message. I kept it short and to the point: *I'm trying to reach Ed Bishop about a private matter. Please return my call.* I left my name and number and hung up.

It had been a long day, and I felt as tired as Rocky appeared to be. I shut down my computer and went upstairs to take a much-needed shower. The hall closet was open, and when I got closer to shut it, I glanced into the spare bedroom and spotted Lily's suitcase on the floor next to the bed. Of course, she'd left it here. When we headed out this morning, we never could have imagined the series of events that unfolded, from Gil's murder to Tex's series of mishaps. If a team of high-spirited boys hadn't inflicted them, I might have thought those events were related.

The most common and least desirable items I acquired through my estate sale purchases were telephones. Western Electric princess phones, Automatic Electric "space maker" 183 phones, ATC Deco-Tel Candlestick phones, donut phones, rotary phones, and wall-mounted phones. Millennials viewed them about as useful as a box of Betamax cartridges. I saw them as the perfect side table accessory for every room in the house, the guest bedroom being no exception.

The room was sparsely decorated. Inside, a bed with a low frame sat on a rectangular sisal rug that partially covered the existing cranberry shag carpeting I'd never pulled up. A minimalistic white side table sat along the wall, holding a vintage green glazed ceramic planter with a waxy red anthurium growing inside it. Alongside the plant was an ivory Ericophone that could have come straight from the set of *The Prisoner.*

I didn't know Lily's cell number, but Tex had benefited from my bounty of telephones, so I called his landline and waited while it rang. A female voice answered, but it wasn't Lily's.

"Allen residence."

"Donna?" I asked.

"I should have figured it was you when this ridiculous phone rang. I didn't even know Tex had a landline."

"What are you doing at Tex's place?"

"Lily called. She told me what happened today and asked if I'd keep her company."

There it was again. The pang of jealousy I felt when Lily turned to Nasty and not me. It was completely irrational—Lily knew me about as well as she knew the cashier at the corner drug store—but I couldn't help it. An existing social network was in place here, and I wasn't part of it.

"Of course," I said. "Is she okay?"

"She's four bottles into a six-pack of Lone Star, so I'd say she's handling things as well as anybody."

"Lily drinks Lone Star too?" I asked.

"It's the official beer of the Allen clan. Are you calling with news about Tex?"

"No. As far as I know, he's either in a drug-induced slumber or making a nuisance of himself to the hospital staff. I'm calling because Lily's overnight bag is still here at my house, and I wanted to see if she needs it."

"Not necessary," Nasty said. "I loaned her what she needed, so she's all set."

"What about the boys?"

"They spent the night here. They already had their overnight bags. Is that it?"

I felt like she was giving me the brush-off. I sank down on the bed amidst sheets that was still unmade from this morning and stared at the suitcase on the floor. Lily didn't seem to care that she'd left it here. "No, that's all," I said. "Tell Lily I'll bring her bag to Mad for Mod tomorrow morning."

"I'll give her the message."

I hung up and stripped the sheets from the bed. When I tossed them onto the floor, a set of pink cotton pajamas fell from between the folds. I picked them up and carried them to Lily's suitcase. I had every intention of undoing the zipper and shoving them inside. I didn't know the zipper was already open or that when I tipped the suitcase, its contents would spill out.

For the second time that day, I ended up on the floor, collecting Lily's personal belongings. She'd packed T-shirts, jeans, sneakers, and a whole lot of racy lingerie, which, for all I knew, was her way of celebrating her body. I refolded the clothes and was about to fit them back into the roller bag when I noticed a mint green folder that had been buried underneath Lily's attire. Curiosity (and a little pain from having been excluded from the impromptu party at Tex's) was calling the shots now. I pulled out the folder and scanned the contents.

It was a life insurance policy. It stated that Lily was to receive a five-million-dollar payout in the event of Gil's death.

Five million dollars.

I'd seen Gil's house. I'd see his place of work. I didn't

know the average income for botanists, but while Gil resisted Lily's requests for divorce, he hadn't been forthcoming with money to make their life more comfortable. Lily had spent her days processing insurance claims from home to keep the boys in jockstraps and milk snakes, and she'd complained more than once about how little Gil contributed to their lifestyle.

I flipped through the papers, scanning them for details that might tell me something else. But the life insurance policy only made up about half of the pages in the folder. The second half was a set of divorce papers.

Lily and Gil's names were spelled out on page one, as was the information about the courthouse, the division of property, and custody of the boys. Before I'd ever met Lily, Tex had told me how she'd been pressuring Gil for this for almost ten years—since shortly after Adam's birth, after he left her with a six-month-old baby and three boys under ten years old. Of everything I knew about Gil, it was that fact that cast him in the most unsympathetic light, and I'd been fully on Lily's side from that moment on.

But one thing bothered me about these papers and it wasn't the signature. It was the phrase written across the page instead: *over my dead body.*

CHAPTER TWELVE

I REACHED UP AND FLICKED ON THE OVERHEAD LIGHT SO I could read the documents more clearly. According to what I was holding, Gil had rejected Lily's request in a way that left little room for misinterpretation. And if that was the case, then what had changed his mind? Had he changed his mind at all? We'd gone to the arboretum to collect the paperwork, but to my knowledge, it never existed.

Why *had* Lily needed to go to the arboretum yesterday morning? The morning we found his body? I froze at the thought, because a second, more alarming one followed on its heels. Had Lily *known* we were going to find Gil's body?

No. That was crazy. Lily wouldn't have—

And then a series of details came back to me. The ringing phone in Gil's pocket and how I'd learned it was Lily on the other end of that call. Nasty's instructions to let her handle the situation. Tex's series of mishaps that kept him from being involved in the ensuing investigation. By then, I'd gone from being the person who discovered Gil's body to a person who'd withheld information, mainly because Tex's words had been ringing in my ears: *family is different.*

But what did that mean?

Here, I was at a disadvantage. Even Nasty understood the Allen code and had acted accordingly. Was her theory about the murderer lingering by while we were there correct? Or had she done something...

No. That was crazy too. Nasty wouldn't have—

I leaned back against the wall and let my hand fall to my lap. What did I really know about the events at the arboretum? I'd been there and felt like I was in the dark. All I really knew was that Gil was dead, poisoned by a toxic plant probably any botanist worth his degree would know not to ingest.

I was surrounded by conflicting information, and the biggest conflict came from when I'd spoken to Tex after finding Gil's body. What had he said? I closed my eyes and searched my memory until I could retrieve his words: *I talked to Lily. She told me what happened. There's nothing to do. Get the divorce papers and leave Gil there.*

Those weren't typical Tex instructions. They had troubled me at the time, but everything about that morning had been checked against his assertion about family. And because I didn't know how that felt, because I'd been operating as a solo unit for more than half of my life, I hadn't questioned it. At the time, I had no way to know that Tex was dealing with a small squadron of pranksters or that his attention had been split between our conversation and the bathroom.

And then something else struck me. I opened my eyes and sat upright. If Lily had talked to Tex, if she'd told him what happened, then she wouldn't have had to tell him at the hospital. He would already have known. But I'd been there when she had. Except... she hadn't.

She told Tex that Gil was dead, but she didn't tell him her ex had been murdered. She didn't mention the police. Tex's question: *have you told the boys?* Her answer: *not yet.* She'd been purposely evasive, and I wanted to know why.

I reached for the phone and started to call Tex's number a second time. I didn't finish dialing.

The thing was, I'd met Gil, and he was every bit the jerk Tex described. I'd walked through the house he left Lily, and I knew it was far from move-in ready. He'd lied about that, but other things weren't adding up either. Not this life insurance policy or the divorce papers, not the notes printed out from Gil's lab that had been in the envelope Lily took this morning, not the truckload of dirt delivered to Lily Banks along with a threat. Not the school transcripts Lily said she'd handed off to the principal but still carried with her.

Lily was in some kind of trouble, and I'd promised Tex I'd look out for her. And that was something I could do.

* * *

AFTER A TROUBLED NIGHT of tortured dreams, I gave up on sleep and got up at five. The sun wouldn't rise for a couple of hours, but that never stopped me before. I showered and dressed in a vintage ensemble from the estate of Barbara Hill. According to Barbara's obituary, she'd been a wife, a mother, and a steno girl, but what she'd most want to be remembered for was playing in the Curtis Cup. Her wardrobe consisted of brightly colored sweaters, Bermuda shorts, and the greatest collection of functional-but-mostly-outdated "skorts" that I'd ever come across. Today's outfit was a yellow pullover with a green daisy pinned to it, a green skort, yellow, green, and white argyle knee socks, and green Keds.

I carried Lily's suitcase downstairs and propped it against the doorframe. I fed Rocky and drank a cup of yesterday's coffee, then wandered to a street-facing window and looked outside at my car. There wasn't enough wind to have carried away the dirt deposited on the hood of my car, so it was up to me to deal with it. I pulled a transparent plastic raincoat over my green and yellow outfit and covered my Keds and argyle socks in disposable blue boot covers I stocked to keep from tracking dirt inside newly decorated interiors. I grabbed an empty jar and lid from my kitchen cabinet, grabbed a broom, and went outside.

A responsible homeowner might have cleaned up the dirt, transferred it to their backyard or garden or, if feeling generous, offered it to their neighbors. I was feeling less generous than tired and annoyed with the unwanted nuisance. But it would have been foolish to pretend this had nothing to do with Gil's murder. I just didn't know what.

I used my empty jar to collect a sample of dirt for the police, which quieted some of the voices that told me I'd been irresponsible, screwed on the lid, and set it inside my car, then picked up the broom and swept the loose dirt from the hood of my car onto the street. I wondered what, exactly, the two men had intended by their stunt. Was dumping this much dirt on a residential street a crime? If Tex had come over after his shift, I would have told him about the incident, not because I expected him to do something about it but because it was one of those unique situations we often talked about at the end of our days. Two men had emptied a truckload of dirt onto my car. I knew how much furniture I could fit into a delivery van—both the weight and the space requirements—but dirt? I had no idea what that would entail.

After I'd cleared enough space to back my car away from the dirt, I removed my raincoat and booties and drove to the house on Cinderella Lane. Granules of dirt that I'd missed with the broom freed themselves as I drove and pelted the windshield. I switched on my wipers to knock them free, careful not to release any wiper fluid, which would just leave behind a muddy mess. It was early enough to beat rush hour. As I turned the corner and headed toward the property, I was concerned to discover a pick-up truck in the driveway. I parked alongside the front property line like I had yesterday. Then, with trepidation, I headed inside to see what inconvenience I'd meet with next.

The front door was open, resting against the chipped white doorframe. I pushed on the door and peeked into the room. Worn shag carpeting had been pulled back from the corner, exposing about four feet of hardwood. A set of leather gloves sat on the carpet next to a carpet puller, a dust mask, and a pair of pliers. The initials J. N. were written on the back of the gloves in a black permanent marker. I recognized the handwriting, and for what felt like the first time in forty-eight hours, I knew the answers to my questions.

"Jimmy?" I called out. "It's Madison."

I ventured farther into the house. The thick carpeting

cloaked my footsteps. It did the same thing for Jimmy, apparently, which was why, when we each turned a corner and faced each other, we jumped like cartoon cats seeing their reflections in a mirror.

Jimmy Nussbaum was my other employee. He was a graduating senior at Lakewood Prep who'd interned with his uncle at a small, privately owned newspaper in downtown Dallas. Among other things on his résumé, Jimmy had the auspicious credit of having reported me as deceased when he mixed up a jazz singer's name with my own—providing ample evidence that he was not destined to work in the newspaper trade. While sorting through the problems that came along with his error, I discovered Jimmy's true passion in life was woodworking. Being something of an opportunistic business owner, I overlooked the fact that he'd given me a premature death and put him on the payroll.

"Jeez, boss, you scared me." He wore a pair of plastic safety goggles held in place with a piece of elastic knotted at the back of his head. His hair was long in the front, and some of his bangs had gotten caught under the goggles. He jerked his head back and to the left in what appeared to be an attempt to shake the hair out of his line of vision. The hair that wasn't caught under the glasses flopped to the side.

I reached over to his head and pulled off the goggles. He smoothed his hair back with his hand and held it on top of his head for a few seconds. It wasn't long enough for a man bun, but it was getting close.

"Don't you have school today?" I asked.

He paused for a moment before answering. "Yeah, but I have first period study hall, so I don't have to be there until a quarter to ten. What time is it?"

I turned around, looking for a clock. The one on the wall had stopped at three thirty. "It's probably still morning," I said. "When did you get here?"

"Four. Effie called me yesterday and told me about the house, and I was too excited to sleep."

Now that we'd gotten past the whole Madison-Night-is-Dead thing, it was hard not to like Jimmy. Offering a high school student a job as my part-time contractor had been risky, but I hadn't once regretted it. He got along well with Effie, which was a bonus. (But I was still adjusting to the whole "hey, boss" thing.)

Not many people saw the potential in a property like this house, but I could tell from the light in Jimmy's eyes (and his inability to sleep last night) that he did. "What did Effie tell you?"

"Just that a new client got bumped up to the top of the calendar. She said you didn't know how bad the structural damage was, and you would need me to do a full walk-through first before you started designing. That's true, right?" He faltered. "She wasn't just pulling my leg, was she?"

"Did she tell you who the client was?"

"No. Why? Is that important?" He glanced around. "I thought maybe one of your existing clients was moving."

"No, this is a new client. She received the house as part of her divorce settlement."

"I hope she got more than the house. Most people would see it as kind of a dump." He looked up at the black-and-white polka-dotted ceiling. "It's going to take a lot of work."

Internally, I weighed the pros and cons of telling Jimmy that the house now belonged to Tex's sister. Jimmy's interactions with Tex thus far hadn't gone smoothly, and that information might prove distracting. But something else stuck with me, something I hadn't considered until now.

"You go to Lakewood Prep, don't you?" Jimmy nodded. "Who's your principal?"

"Mr. Rich."

"Franklin Rich?"

"Yeah. Why?" The sudden change in conversation made Jimmy uneasy. "Are you going to report me for something?"

"Report you for what? You just told me you have first period study hall, and you don't have to be at school until nine forty-five."

Jimmy's face turned red. He looked down at his shoes and mumbled something I didn't hear, except for the last word, which was "suspended."

"Jimmy, what did you do?"

He averted his eyes. "It wasn't my fault."

I couldn't imagine what Jimmy had done to get suspended, but he was my employee, and if he'd engaged in some troublesome behavior, I needed to know. "Jimmy?"

"I got caught eating brownies."

"What kind of brownies?" I asked. There was only one kind of brownie I figured a high school student would get suspended for eating, but I wanted to hear Jimmy say it.

"Baseball brownies."

His reply left me temporarily at a loss for words. When I spoke, it was to ask, "What are baseball brownies?"

He looked up. "Trish McCardell brought in brownies for the baseball team. She had four trays of them! And I had a tuna sandwich for lunch because I thought Amber was out sick, but she came to school after lunch, and I'd been wanting to ask her out, but my breath smelled like fish, so I took one."

That was a lot of information. I often forgot how much teenagers had to say.

"You took one of the brownies? That Trish McCardell intended for the baseball team? To mask your tuna breath?"

"Yeah," he said. He wasn't nearly as impressed as I was at having kept up with his narrative. "Somebody saw me take it and told Principal Rich and he suspended me."

"For how many days?"

"Three." He pushed his hair out of his face again.

Three days suspension for eating a brownie intended for the baseball team? "That seems like an excessive punishment."

"Principal Rich is on a witch hunt ever since two kids were caught dealing drugs behind the school."

"Swiping brownies is a far cry from dealing drugs."

"That's what I said!" Jimmy exclaimed. He made a tight fist. "I'd like to punch him in the face."

I assessed Jimmy, all one-hundred-twenty pounds of him, and stifled a smile. "Violence never solved anything," I said instead.

"Are you going to fire me?"

"Why would I fire you? You just told me you've got three full days to work on this property. I don't really see a downside."

Jimmy shifted his eyes from the floor to the wall behind me. His lack of eye contact was suspicious.

"Jimmy? What's the downside?"

"There's a new guy starting at my school. Girls always like the new guy."

"Give Amber the benefit of the doubt. Maybe she likes bad boys," I said. This got his attention. I added an explanation. "You were suspended. You're officially a bad boy now."

"Really?" he asked with more than a trace of hope. "Do you think I should get a black leather jacket?"

I scanned Jimmy's gray hoodie, faded jeans, and knee pads. "I think you should be you."

He scanned my green and yellow vintage golf outfit. "Figures you'd say that."

Our conversation had taken a turn from where it had started, but I'd gotten one vital piece of information. Assuming only one Franklin Rich worked in the Dallas school systems (which seemed a fair assumption), then Jimmy's principal was the house call-making driver of the red Lexus who'd been at my house. I was more than a little curious about him, mostly because Lily hadn't exactly been on the up and up about his visit.

Now that I knew I had Jimmy for longer than the few pre-school hours I'd originally thought, I put my questions about his principal on the back burner and shifted gears to more pressing matters.

"I'll let you get back to your work in a moment, but did you sign for a delivery from the powder coater yesterday?"

"Yeah. I had them put the fixtures in the satellite storage by your house."

"When?"

"Yesterday around lunch. Effie said you did that with the other delivery, so I just assumed that's what we were doing now."

The other delivery. With everything that had happened since Lily arrived, I'd forgotten all about the cartons that had arrived from my parents' estate. I wouldn't have noticed the delivery from the powder coater even if I had been inside my satellite office; the newly painted fixtures had probably been added to the stack of boxes I'd pretended didn't exist. I'd been so interested in finding a distraction to keep my pent-up emotions at bay.

"When you want to take a break, can you deliver them to the Greenville showroom? I'd like to use them in the spring window display with the pink Pyrex."

He removed his plastic safety goggles from his head and tossed them on top of the rest of his tools. "I'll do it now. I need to get a few more tools anyway." He headed toward the front door but stopped and turned back. "You sure are cool."

Despite the house's condition, the bones were solid. It was a brick exterior with slab foundation. The interior had three bedrooms, three full bathrooms, a fireplace, and a den. I'd suggest to Lily that we convert the den into a bedroom for David, her oldest. She could give George his own room, too, and Adam and Gabe would bunk together. When David headed off to college in the fall, each boy would get his own space.

Gil had interesting taste in decorating. The walls of the master bedroom were covered with wood paneling, and the carpet was thick green shag. His idea of move-in ready included a double bed and a built-in walnut table/dresser/shelf unit along one wall.

I wandered over to the fixture. Rectangles of dust remained behind on the wood, indicating that books or something similar had been here and removed. I blew on the surface, and small fibers floated through the air, picking up light from the window and slowly falling to the ugly green carpet. Something jutted out from underneath the fixture's base, and I bent down and judged it out with the toe of my sneaker.

The object was a spiral-bound calendar. The cover read Lakewood Arboretum, and the dates matched this year. The corners of the cover were dinged up, showing signs of wear. I flipped it open, and the front page said Gil Banks followed by a phone number. I pulled out my cell and checked my call log. It was the same number I'd called last night that I'd gotten from the arboretum website. I tried the call again, and again, no one answered. I disconnected the call, my curiosity spinning off into a new direction.

I closed Gil's notebook and turned it over in my hands. The only things left behind for Lily were items Gil appeared to have purposely discarded, either junk or jokes. The dust on the shelving unit indicated he'd even taken the books that had been there for display. He might not have known he dropped this calendar. So, what had Gil been up to in the days leading up to his murder? There was one way to find out.

CHAPTER THIRTEEN

I OPENED THE CALENDAR AND SCANNED THE DATES. A recurring appointment was written on every Wednesday, starting the third week in January, and continuing through June: SD, 7:00.

I wasn't sure where I'd find Lily, so I called my studio first.

"Mad for Mod," she answered.

"Lily? It's Madison."

"Hey, girl," she said, which was a far cry from "hey, boss," though "hey" seemed to transcend generational lines. "What's up?"

I was still troubled by the documents I'd found in Lily's suitcase. They were none of my business, but their presence felt like a Sputnik lamp with extra rods—extra information that Lily had wanted to suppress. I pushed my lingering concerns over Lily aside.

"I'm at the house on Cinderella Lane," I said. "I found a calendar in the bedroom. I think it belonged to Gil."

"And?"

"And there's a recurring appointment on the third Wednesday of every month. 'SD.' Do you know who that might be?"

"SD?" she repeated. She was silent for a few beats, during which I pictured her thinking over Gil's acquaintances, trying to come up with a match. After a stretch of silence, she said, "Madison? Are you still there?"

"Yes, I was waiting for you."

"For what?"

"To tell me if the letters 'SD' means anything to you."

"San Diego?"

"Did Gil have business in San Diego? Did he go there weekly?"

"How should I know?"

"I was hoping—"

"Madison, I don't think you fully understand the scope of my life. I have four boys in the public school system. That means I'm up at six, not because I like getting up at six but because from six to seven is the only time the house is quiet. The boys are up at seven, and then I get them off to school by eight. I work from home processing insurance claims until four thirty, when they get home from baseball practice, and from that point it's dinner, milk snakes, and homework until they go to bed. If Gil was flying to California every week, he sure wasn't going to tell me."

I set the calendar on the closest shelf and ran my finger down the page. Other notations were scribbled here and there, the kind of things that occupied most calendars: doctor's appointments, car service, important anniversaries. A flight from Dallas to San Diego would take about three hours, not impossible on an in-and-out trip, but weekly? That implied an importance to the trip, possibly a regular meeting. I didn't understand enough about botany to know what kind of regular meetings Gil may have had, but today was Wednesday, and the only thing I was sure about was that Gil wouldn't make his standing appointment. The question seemed to be not so much about what he was doing but whether the person he was doing it with knew he wasn't going to show.

"I'll let the cops know. This might help them move on to a different angle." I closed the calendar. "And just a heads' up. Jimmy, my teenaged handyman, is going to stop by with a pair of pink kitchen appliances to use in the window with the Pyrex."

"I sold the Pyrex yesterday."

"I don't mean a set of Pyrex, I mean the cart we filled yesterday."

"Right. You had a walk-in. She saw the cart and bought it all." She paused. "It was all priced in the inventory system so I assumed it was for sale. I have her contact information if you need to reach her."

"No. You were right. It's all for sale. I've just never had a customer walk in and buy four figures worth of mixing bowls before."

"She said she has a popular internet cooking show and wanted to use them on her new set. She's planning to cook her way through the Betty Crocker cookbook in June and said her audience would flip."

Somewhere over the past decade, there had been a shift in desirability for mid-century modern design. When I first started Mad for Mod, my clientele was rooted in nostalgia, having grown up around the styles, or discovering them through old movies and TV shows. These days, a new audience had discovered the novelty of mid-mod and leveraged the kitsch factor as a banner of individuality. My clients tended toward the former, not the latter, but a savvy businesswoman does not turn up her nose at a walk-in customer who just paid the rent on her storefront. In fact...

"You said you have her contact information?" Lily affirmed that she did. "Follow up and see if she'd be interested in a newly refurbished oven, range top, and dishwasher powder-coated to match the Pyrex." I named a price that gave me a tidy profit but was far below what companies who produced retro kitchen equipment would charge for the same appliances.

"What do you want me to do about the window?"

"I'll handle it later today. That reminds me. Did Donna tell you I have your overnight bag? I can bring it to the studio or drop it by Tex's place."

"Save yourself a trip," she said. "Just bring it to Donna's tonight."

"What's at Donna's?"

"The cookout," she said.

"What cookout?"

"Donna's hosting a party to welcome us to Dallas. She thought it would be fun for the boys to have a cookout. It should be a good distraction."

"Right." Was it me, or was no one acting in a manner that suited the circumstances? "What time is Donna's thing?"

"Around six. You close at five, right? I left David in charge of his brothers, so I'll get them all from Tex's place and meet you there."

"Yes, five is good."

"Another call is coming in. See you later, Madison." She hung up on me before I could say goodbye.

The day was shaping up differently than I'd expected, but if I wanted business to continue as usual, I'd have to fit a new window display into my schedule.

I dismissed the feeling that Nasty and Lily were up to something to which I wasn't privy. It wasn't the first time I'd felt the two of them handling things on their own. While I trusted Nasty to get results in just about any situation, I couldn't clearly define what results she wanted to get in this case. The feeling of high school hung over everything since Lily and the boys arrived—jealousy, envy, cliquishness. I already knew how I wanted to live my life. I was too old for those games.

Of the possible three calls to make, I called the police. Specifically, I called Sue's direct number.

"Niedermeier," Sue answered.

"Sue, hi, it's Madison."

"Hey. Any word on Captain Allen?"

"Not yet," I said, not sure if I'd know if there was. "That's not why I'm calling. I may have information relating to Gil Banks's murder."

"Where are you?"

"I'm in the house he left Lily."

"Midway Hills, right?"

"Right. End of the cul-de-sac on Cinderella Lane. I'll leave the front door unlocked." I gave her the house number and hung up.

While I waited for Sue and her partner to arrive, I continued my walk-through. The curtains had been drawn yesterday, casting funky shadows across the carpet and the few pieces of furniture Gil had left behind so he could call the place "move-in ready." Someone—presumably Jimmy— had pulled up the blinds in the kitchen, but the bedrooms were still cloaked in darkness. With each room I entered, I opened the blinds and curtains to allow in natural light then pushed open the windows to allow in fresh air. I carried a sketchpad with me and took notes while I walked: *repaint interiors, replace closet doors, space theme for David, vintage baseball pennants for Adam/Gabe.* I briefly wondered if a seventies-era poster of Farrah Fawcett would be acceptable for George's room or if that would just throw fuel onto a fire.

As I walked the house, I formed an opinion about more than its decorating needs. I didn't have to meet Gil to know I didn't like him. From the cheap seats, it looked like he took Lily for granted from the moment they married, and he'd also stood in the way of her leaving him. His boys had grown up without a father, picking up habits here and there, and Lily had been left with limited choices about having a fulfilling relationship of her own if she wanted a fair divorce. Everything I'd learned about Gil from the get-go told me he had some sort of hold on her. She didn't seem like the type to roll over and play dead, but she'd let almost ten years of her life pass instead of fighting him for her freedom. Even *she* didn't appear to trust herself around him. Gil was like Charles Manson with plants.

The next bedroom was no better. Thick rust-colored carpeting picked up the least attractive shade in a bold floral wallpaper that reminded me of a Laura Ashley dress I'd once worn in college. Even the decorator seemed to have been on the fence regarding the print. Two walls were fully covered, and the remaining two included only the pattern used as a border.

The third bedroom was the most neutral. Ivory carpet, ivory walls, and an ivory bedspread. A mirror hung mounted to one wall, reflecting the light that came in from the windows over the bed.

I filled several pages with notes while I walked through the house. My initial reaction had proven correct: ninety percent of the interior would have to go. The remaining ten percent made up the three bathrooms: one pink, one blue, and one yellow. I was a sucker for a colored bathroom, and this house did not disappoint. I doubted the boys would agree.

Sue arrived sans partner. She found me standing in the kitchen, staring up at the polka-dotted ceiling, and announced her presence with a low whistle. "What makes someone put polka-dotted wallpaper on a kitchen ceiling?"

"Contentious divorce proceedings?" I said without thinking. Then I added, "Or maybe he just had unique taste."

"Right." She shook her head at the decorating choice. "Is Ms. Banks here?"

"No. She's covering the phones at my studio while I work here."

Sue nodded and then looked around the place again. "Is this a legitimate job or a favor for Captain Allen?"

"A little bit of both, I suppose. I told Lily she could have her pick of my inventory at cost, but she was going to have Gil pay my rate." My voice trailed off as I considered what the last twenty-four hours meant for me. I didn't mind doing this job for Lily—she was Tex's sister, after all, and anybody could see she deserved a break in life—but for a company that operated with two and a half employees, allocating my assets to a nonpaying gig wasn't the smartest move.

"She's got boys, right?" Sue asked. "Maybe they can help."

"Three of them are under the legal working age."

"I won't tell if you won't," she said with a wink.

I liked Sue. She was easy to talk to and, more often than not, felt like a friend. She and her partner, Ling, had been hired during a challenging time at the Lakewood Police Department. There'd been a growing rift between the public and the police, and Tex understood the more he could improve community relations, the more effective his team could be. He hired them both during a recruiting phase intended to make the Lakewood Police Department reflect the community, and Sue and Ling had been so successful in getting confessions that they now traveled the country, teaching classes on their methods. They inspired their own meme: "You've been Sued!" One of the patrol cops had printed the saying on T-shirts, which the department sold at a recent chili cook-off. The LPD didn't win the chili contest, but they made enough in T-shirt sales to buy a fancy espresso machine for the precinct, allowing Mr. Coffee a long-overdue retirement.

"So," Sue said, "you have some information for me?"

"Yes." I led her to the bedroom. While I retrieved the calendar, Sue scanned the room.

"What a dump," she said. "If I were Mrs. Banks, I'd ditch this place and buy a condo."

"Are you kidding me? This is an unrenovated 1957 ranch house. Do you know how hard it is these days to find a mid-century ranch that hasn't been flipped?"

"Doesn't that tell you something?"

"It tells me television is ruining the world as we know it."

"You're showing your age, Madison."

I laughed. She wasn't wrong.

Then I picked up the calendar from the shelf. "I found this under the shelving unit. There's enough dust on the shelf to show Gil kept books there, books that had recently been removed. I don't think he knew he left this behind." I flipped the calendar open then turned it so it was facing Sue, and I pointed at the recurring appointment on Wednesdays. "I asked Lily if she knew what that was, and she seemed to think it was San Diego."

"Did he have a history of going there?"

"I don't know."

"But she did?"

"She said that was the only SD she knew of. I don't think she knew a lot about his life here, so it could have been an educated guess."

"Right." Sue took the calendar from me and flipped to the previous month and the month before that. "The appointments started in January." She flipped back to April and then turned the page to May. "Nothing on here for next month."

"Maybe he didn't have a chance to update the calendar."

"Maybe," she said, though it didn't feel like she was agreeing with me. "He was starting a new job, wasn't he?"

"Yes. In New Zealand. Maybe the trips to San Diego were related to his research here, and he doesn't have to go there anymore."

"Could be." Sue closed the calendar. "Does Mrs. Banks know you called me?"

"Yes. I checked with her first to see if she knew Gil's schedule, and then I told her I was going to call you next."

She handed the calendar back to me. "Thanks."

"Don't you want to keep it?"

"Not your property to give."

"Right." I set the calendar back on the shelf. I doubted Lily would care if Sue took it, but it stood out that Sue was treating this calendar like the property of a person of interest.

"Do you have any leads?" I asked.

"A couple. I'd love to talk to the business partner to find out what he and Mr. Banks were working on, but we still haven't been able to reach him."

"Does that bother you?"

"Truthfully? Yes. I've got a victim found dead at his place of work. I've talked to the arboretum manager, who said he didn't even know Mr. Banks installed a security alarm. Technically, that violates the contract they signed with the arboretum, but if Nasty hadn't gone out there to investigate the alarm, Gil Banks might still be lying on the floor of his lab."

"Nobody's looking for him?"

She held her hands up. "Gil Banks was a ghost. He had no friends, no personal life, no regular hangouts. This is the address he had on file, but nothing here can inform us of his life. If you hadn't told me about the job in New Zealand, I'd say the man was getting ready to disappear."

CHAPTER FOURTEEN

I STARED AT SUE WHILE HER WORDS SANK IN. EVERYTHING that had happened regarding Gil Banks took on a different hue, like someone tweaked the settings in Photoshop and gave it all a distorted shade.

"What if he was?" I asked. Sue raised her eyebrows, and I continued. "Tex's sister has been asking him for a divorce for nine years and he finally agreed. What happened to change his mind? This new job—aside from him telling Lily about it —has anyone found any evidence that it exists? What about a new relationship? Do we know anything about Gil Banks that's been confirmed?"

Sue shook her head.

"I have something else that might help you. Follow me." I led Sue out the front door to my car and removed the small jar of dirt from inside. "Two men pulled up in a van in front of my studio this morning. I was with Lily. They dumped a vanload of dirt onto the hood of my car." I held out the jar.

"This is a sample?"

"Yes, but to be honest, I lacked the proper motivation to clean up my side of the street, so the rest of it is probably still there."

Sue unscrewed the lid and sniffed the contents, then held it up to the sun. Satisfied that it was, indeed, dirt, she screwed the cap back on. "I'll have the lab run it and see if there's anything to be learned from it, but if these men dumped a whole vanload of it, I doubt they were worried it could be traced back to them. Did they say anything?"

"They said it was her turn to step up. They mentioned the business."

"I thought Mr. Banks worked for the arboretum?"

"That's what I thought too, but it does seem that there's more to Gil Banks than meets the eye."

Sue checked that the lid of the jar of dirt was secure and dropped it into her suit jacket pocket. "I can see what Captain Allen sees in you. You look at things differently. Are you sure you don't want to change careers?" she asked.

This wasn't the first time one of the detectives in Tex's precinct had noticed I had a natural ability to look at a case differently than most civilians, and while I appreciated the compliment, I also felt guilty for not being forthcoming from the beginning. Although I relished the opportunity to steer Sue's investigation away from Lily and onto Gil's possible secret life, I was eager to catch Tex up on the full scope of the situation before saying something that might put Lily deeper into the investigation.

"Unless police work comes with a paintbrush, I'm sticking with decorating."

I walked Sue to the front door.

"Thanks for the dirt," she said, "and for the tip about the

calendar. That information might send the investigation into a whole new direction. I'll check with the arboretum and see if they know anything about Mr. Banks's trips to San Diego, and I'll get Jerry to check the airport manifests. A couple of rookies are at the precinct, going over the victim's credit card statements. Hopefully, we'll find something."

"Good, old-fashioned police work."

"Keeps us honest."

Sue left. I turned around and headed to the sliding doors at the back of the house. I pulled the blinds open to allow in sunlight and get a clear view of the backyard. The day was becoming gorgeous. I slid the back door open and went outside to check out the yard. The patio was big enough for a grill and seating area. A small green gardening shed with a rusted padlock on the door sat on the edge of the property. The yard was in great shape, which didn't surprise me, considering Gil's experience with plants. He may have let the interior of the house fall into disrepair, but he appeared to have done yard work up to the very end. The lawn was a crisp, even shade of bright Kelly green. Gardening tools were propped along the exterior of the shed, and a small garden housed several tall, conical metal frames that protected tomato plants from hungry critters.

The front door to the house behind Lily's opened, and an old man walked out. He wore medium-blue overalls, and his face was tan and weathered, the skin of someone who spent a lifetime in the sun. "You the buyer?" he called out.

"The buyer of what?"

He pointed at the house. "The property. I heard it changed hands recently. Saw that kid show up this morning and figured I was going to meet my new neighbors today."

"Nope, I'm the decorator. Madison Night."

The man approached the fence and hung his arms down on Lily's side of it. "Surprised you that I knew somebody bought the place, didn't it? I saw it in your face. Hope she didn't pay too much."

What Lily had paid for the house wasn't a price that banks recognized as a down payment, but how she acquired the property was her business, not mine, so I didn't respond to her neighbor's assumption. "Some people fall in love with the bones of a house and can see past the temporary décor."

"That's not what happened here. The guy who owned this place didn't live in it. He didn't care about the inside of the house."

"Wasn't he a botanist?" I asked. "It makes sense that he would care about his landscaping."

"Landscaping. Right. Is that what you call gardening at midnight?"

I stopped to think about that. If Gil's murder had something to do with the property he left Tex's sister, that would come back to haunt her. I fought the urge to glance back at the freshly tended vegetable garden. If Gil had been doing something shady back here, he hadn't done a great job of covering it up.

"I'm sorry. I didn't catch your name," I said.

"Didn't catch it because I didn't give it. Name's Harry."

"Have you lived next to Gil a long time?"

"I've been here since this development was built. Watched the whole neighborhood turn over, some houses more than once. Couples move in, have families, move out. If Banks lived here, I'd have known it. He thought he was being quiet with his midnight gardening, but I heard him. That guy has a secret, I tell you."

I approached the fence. "Have you ever peeked over the fence to find out what Gil was planting back here?" I asked. I gave Harry my broadest smile and hoped my friendly demeanor would keep him chatting.

He scowled. "I'm not one of those *Rear Window* types. You can't expect others to respect your privacy if you go poking into theirs," he said.

For all of Harry's initial charm, he had a no-BS manner. I usually found it refreshing to talk to people who were direct. You knew where they stood. But Harry made me feel like I was being challenged. He claimed he valued his privacy and left others alone so they'd reciprocate, but he'd been the one who introduced the idea of Gil's late-night activities into the conversation. Harry had known about the property changing hands. And the whole time, he'd kept very direct eye contact with me, almost as if I were the one bringing an unsavory element to the community.

"Well, I won't keep you," he said. "New owner is probably paying you by the hour and not my place to run up his bill."

"It's a her," I said. At his confused expression, I clarified. "The new owner. She's a single mother with four boys."

"You don't say."

"I'm sure you'll meet them soon." I gestured back at the house. "Nice chatting with you, Harry." I pointed over his fence at a white, weather-beaten rocking chair on his patio. "A light sanding and a fresh coat of paint will revive that rocker," I said, mostly to let him know I noticed things too.

My conversation with Harry had run its course, so I headed back to the house. Once safely back inside, I turned around and slid the back door closed. Harry was still watching me from over the top of his fence.

As far as the job was concerned, I knew I needed a concept for the house. But as much as I wanted to push everything out of my mind and decorate this place from end to end, my attention kept getting pulled back to Gil and Lily.

I dropped into the torn beanbag chair and kicked my feet out in front of me. I'd been hoping to get a jump on the day, but already it was after eight. I felt the lack of sleep in my body, my joints stiff and my muscles tired. I pulled my phone out of my pocket and found the number for the local high school, then called in and asked for the principal's office. It was as good of an excuse as any to remain seated in the beanbag.

"Lakewood Prep," answered a male voice.

"Hello," I said. "I'm calling for Principal Rich. Is he available?"

"He's not in the office. May I take a message?"

Leaving a message without the context of my relationship to Lily or her boys seemed counterproductive, so I asked when he would return.

"I don't know," the man said. "One of the students thought it would be funny to release a bunch of live frogs in the science lab. He's going to be tied up for a while."

I said I'd call back later and disconnected. I was silently thankful that Lily's boys hadn't yet started at the school, while also recognizing they were going to fit in just fine.

My next call was to the hospital. The front desk informed me that Tex had been released earlier that morning. I called his cell next, not sure where I'd find him.

"Yo, Night," he said. His voice was more alert than the last time we'd spoken.

"How are you feeling?"

"Like a pincushion," he said. "I think they gave me a shot for every bee sting."

"At least you got your S's back," I said. "Those shots may have made the difference between me conversing with you and me conversing with the coroner."

"Pick me out a pretty coffin, okay? Something lined in hunter green."

"Oh, no. It's yellow and white gingham for you, Captain Allen. I'll definitely want the world to see your softer side."

"At least put me in a cowboy hat."

Though the subject was ominous, it was good to hear a lighter tone in Tex's voice. "Where are you?" I asked. "The hospital said they sent you home."

"I'm at your place. Mine's a little crowded."

I stifled a smile. Lily's boys had rendered Tex useless after two days. Anybody would choose to stay somewhere else.

"Have you eaten lunch?" I asked.

"Just got here. Your fridge is empty."

"Any requests?"

"Surprise me."

I grabbed my keys and drove to a strip mall. I parked in front of a chain restaurant that promised a wide selection of soups and salads, where I bought three quarts of various broth-based soups (minestrone, egg drop, and chicken noodle), a package of soup crackers, and a six-pack of ginger ale. I stopped at the grocery store next door and added a rotisserie chicken and a six-pack of Lone Star Beer, which was probably closer to what Tex would want.

The backseat was covered in piles of dry cleaning and crates of bottles to be dropped off at the local recycling plant, but all that could wait. I set the food on the passenger seat and drove to Thelma Johnson's house. Tex was on my sofa with Rocky, half covered in a faded patchwork quilt, watching an episode of *Bosch*.

I set the food down, approached him, and put my hand on his forehead. "Are you feeling okay now? No new symptoms?"

He glared at me. "Who are you? Madison Nightingale?"

I stepped back. "Is it wrong of me to care about how you're feeling?"

He shifted his gaze to somewhere behind me, seemed to think about my question, and shrugged. "Does one of those bags have a little nurse's costume?"

I sighed. "And here I thought a severe allergic reaction to a swarm of bees would slow you down."

He leaned back and folded his hands behind his head. "Not on your life, Night."

"I brought soup." I carried the bags to the kitchen and unpacked the plastic takeout containers, the ginger ale, the beer, the chicken, and the crackers. My personal decorating style veered toward the atomic end of mid-century design, and I often rotated items from my inventory through my house. I pulled two white "Fire King" Anchor Hocking bowls out of my cabinet. They were white milk glass, adorned with stylized gray starbursts in varying sizes, and highlighted with abstracted dots that mimicked a trail of stars. Each bowl had a handle, which would have made carrying easy if I hadn't already stacked everything onto a portable tray.

"I got minestrone, egg drop, and chicken noodle. I don't

know your preference. I admit egg drop is a weird one, but you do like Chinese food." I turned around and checked to see if Tex could still hear me.

He was looking at me funny. This far into knowing him, I felt like I knew how to read his expressions: anger, attraction, flirtation, and his secret weapon, the cop mask. But this one was new. It was softer than usual. His mouth was open slightly, and its sides were turned down. The swelling was mostly gone from his face, and the discoloration of his black eye had faded to a yellowish green. The lines I sometimes saw on his forehead when he was confused or angry were absent. I felt like I was looking at a hint of the boy Tex had been before he had to take care of everybody else.

"Well?" I asked. "Which one do you want?"

"Egg drop," he said.

"One bowl of egg drop soup coming up." I poured some broth into the bowl and scooped out some of the eggs, pepper, tofu, and scallions. I opened a can of ginger ale, assembled the bowl, the can, the spoon, and a napkin on a tray, and carried them all to Tex.

I hadn't realized how hungry I was, and for a few minutes, the only sounds in the living room were those of two adults slurping soup like kids. I wasn't sure which one of us would talk about Gil first. Tex wasn't averse to talking with me about his cases as long as sharing the information wouldn't compromise his investigation, but we hadn't talked much about Gil thanks in large part to the boys—or maybe Tex just wanted me to think that. Maybe he was milking the whole situation to keep me from asking questions about an investigation that fell a little too close to home.

I knew the longer I waited to tell him about my conversation with Sue, the worse it would be, but there was something soft about sick Tex, something less antagonistic that I hadn't experienced before, and I was surprised to discover that I liked it.

Tex ate the soup, keeping one eye on the TV. The whole scene was equal parts domestic and horror movie, which explained my somewhat inappropriate non sequitur.

"I found a calendar at the house today. I don't think Gil knew he left it behind. I called Sue and had her—"

"Niedermeier?" Tex asked.

"Yes. She's the lead detective on the case, right?"

"What case?'

I stared at him. "What kind of drugs did they put you on?"

"What case?" he repeated.

"Gil Banks's murder."

Tex dropped his spoon. "Banks was murdered?"

I set my spoon deliberately. Tex and I stared deep into each other's eyes, but nothing about the moment was romantic. Silence stretched and distorted, like a comic strip pressed onto Silly Putty and manipulated. I grasped for pieces of our conversation from the day I'd found Gil's body.

"I called you," I said. "From the arboretum. Don't you remember? You told me not to worry about Gil and to get Lily out of there."

"What did you do, Night?"

"I gave Lily my keys and told her to come here, and I stayed behind to call the police. But I saw a Big Bro Security sticker on one of the windows—"

Tex interrupted me. "Nasty knows about this?"

"Yes. She's been a big help. She's been keeping your sister company."

Tex pushed his bowl away. The sudden movement sent soup sloshing over the edge. Tex stood and took a few steps, and then he put his hand on the wall to steady himself. I jumped up and wrapped my arm around his waist, and he tried to shake me off, but I could tell he wasn't fully himself.

"It's the painkillers," he said. He shook me off and kept his hand on the wall. He put one hand over his eyes, and I waited for him to storm out. Then he slowly dropped his hand from his eyes. When he looked at me, I saw his pupils were dilated. "I'm mad," he said, though he kept his voice level. "I want to storm out of here and find Lily and lock her in a room to keep her safe. I want to throw Nasty into a jail cell for obstruction of justice."

"What about me?" I asked, not sure I wanted to hear the answer.

What I wanted didn't matter. Tex turned an unflattering shade of green, turned his back to me, and threw up in the vintage metal wastepaper basket in the corner.

CHAPTER FIFTEEN

I PUT MY HANDS ON TEX AND GUIDED HIM BACK TO THE SOFA. He dropped onto the threadbare cushion and closed his eyes. I gently pressed my palm against his forehead. "You're burning up," I said.

He pushed my hand away, but the energy he expended in doing so appeared to wipe him out. I went to the kitchen and ran cool water over a daisy-printed dish towel, which I then carried back to Tex and pressed against his forehead. I expected him to roll his eyes or fight me on the gesture, but he put his hand on top of mine and held the towel in place. This felt like new territory for both of us, and I had no idea what to say.

"I need your help," he said in a voice so quiet I didn't think I'd heard him clearly.

"What?"

He peered up at me. "Don't take advantage of the situation by pretending you didn't hear me." He managed only a faint impression of his normally flirtatious tone, enough for me to hear the tease in it.

I sat down. "It sounded like you asked for my help. Forgive me for wanting to clarify, but it's not something I hear from you every day."

This time the corners of Tex's mouth turned up. A small victory, even if his smile didn't reach his eyes.

I picked up his right hand, set it on top of the damp towel, and then repositioned myself so I was facing him. "Unofficial Lakewood Police Department investigator reporting for duty. What's my assignment, Captain?"

"First assignment is to tell me everything I don't already know."

"I don't know what you know."

"Pretend I don't know anything. Give me the highlights and we'll go from there."

* * *

IT WASN'T until I recapped the past seventy-two hours for Tex that I realized how much had transpired while he was dealing with various health issues, and not until I repeated the details of that first phone call to Tex after finding Gil's body did I discover just how much a small communication glitch could blow things up.

"I called you from the arboretum," I said. "You said you talked to Lily, and she told you what happened. I asked you what to do, and you said there was nothing to do. You said to get the divorce papers and leave."

"And that didn't seem off to you?"

"Whoa, there, Captain. Don't put this on me."

"Have I ever told you to leave a crime scene?"

"She's your *sister*," I said. "Your *family*. You keep saying family is different."

"She didn't kill him." He hesitated, as if wondering whether she could have. "How did she react?"

"She kicked him."

"She what?"

"She kicked him. I told her to wait in the car, but she came into his lab and saw his body. She pushed past me and kicked him and called him a jerk."

Tex shook his head. "Did she leave any clues behind?"

"No. There was an envelope with her name on it propped by the computer. She took it. When she showed me the contents later, they weren't the divorce papers she expected to find."

"What was in the envelope?"

"Research. Recently printed pages of notes about botany." I closed my eyes for a moment, thought back to that day, then opened my eyes. "They still smelled like ink. When I talked to Sue, she something was recently deleted from the computer hard drive."

"Did you tell her about the envelope?"

I averted my eyes. "No." When Tex didn't chastise me, I added, "Sue said the file might still be in the printer buffer."

"You said it was plant research?"

"He was a botanist. Nasty said his research was privately funded. Botany sounds so, I don't know, peaceful. People talking to plants, splicing seeds, and creating new hybrid roses for the bridal market."

"It's gotten a little more political than that," Tex said.

"How can botany be political?"

"The environment is a hot potato for a lot of prospective candidates. Server farms are popping up all over Dallas, and environmentalists are up in arms. Lily said Gil and his partner were approached by a mayoral candidate about genetically mutating plants."

"For what?"

"Something about discovering ways to speed up oxygen production to offset carbon emissions."

"That sounds like science fiction."

"A lot of big breakthroughs start out that way. What does Ed Bishop say?"

It took me a moment to remember the call I'd made to the Lakewood Arboretum in an attempt to talk to Gil's research partner. "No one's been able to reach him."

Tex took a labored breath and held out his hand. "Give me a phone."

I picked up a white donut phone from an end table, shook the cord loose, then held the whole unit out to Tex. At the look on his face, I raised my eyebrows. "It's this or nothing."

He took the phone and called a number from memory.

"It's Captain Allen," Tex said. "What do you have on the Banks case?" He glanced up at me and held his finger over his lips. I nodded and carried the tray of soup bowls into the kitchen.

It was a quarter to five. Nasty's cookout was scheduled for six, which gave me a pocket of time to do something about my showroom windows if I didn't dally. But Tex didn't seem to be in any shape for a party, especially not around Lily's pack of hooligans. I wasn't even sure he'd be okay on his own.

Maternal feelings for me had manifested around animals.

I loved Rocky like he was my son, and I felt the same way about every one of the puppies he sired, including Wojciehowitcz, the troublemaker Shi-Chi that Tex had adopted. But taking care of anybody other than myself, men included, had never held any allure for me. Perhaps that was why I was fifty-two and single.

Make that fifty-two, single, and happy.

But that whole older and wiser thing isn't just a cliché. And you don't really see it coming either. One day, you're completely independent, eschewing advances from the opposite sex, doting on your dog, and building your empire in shades of paint popular during a simpler time. And then *boom!* You find yourself attracted to the most inconvenient man on the planet—a comical twist of fate lifted from the same Doris Day movies that inspired your dining room. Let's just say I didn't ask for this. But when it hit me in the face, I wasn't blind to the possibilities.

As Tex conversed with his detective, I dug my cell phone out of my handbag and called Effie.

"Hey, boss," she said.

"Hi. How'd it go with Nasty today?"

"It was… good?"

"You're not sure?"

"It was good. Different. Nasty isn't what I expected. How were things at your studio?"

"Good. Lily sold our entire inventory of Pyrex while I was at the Cinderella house."

"She told me."

"When did you talk to her?"

"She called Big Bro to get directions for the cookout."

"Right," I said. "Are you… were you planning to go?"

"Me? Why would I be there?" she asked. "It's a party for Lily and her boys."

"I thought Nasty might have invited you."

"No, she left early to go shopping for tonight. Do you need me to help you with a new window display? I'm going to leave here soon."

"No, I'm already at home. I'm about to ask one of those questions employers generally don't ask their employees."

"Shoot."

"Are you available to watch Captain Allen tonight?"

* * *

TEX WASN'T happy about my plan. "She's twenty-six," he said.

"Yes. She is twenty-six. And I trust her with Rocky and with my business. She's met your sister, and she spent her day working with Nasty. If anything happens, she's particularly suited to run interference in several different directions. I can't imagine a better person to keep you company tonight."

"You could have dropped me off at Jumbos," he said with a glimmer in his eyes.

"Yes. Or I could make one of those rigs like Jane Fonda used on Dabney Coleman in *9 to 5*."

"Save that idea for when I'm better."

I threw a pillow at him. "If I didn't know any better, I'd say this is all an act."

"I could probably manage a few moves," he said. His face turned green again, and he grabbed the damp towel and held it to his forehead. "Maybe not."

While waiting for Effie to arrive, I sketched out a new

window. I still wanted a spring concept, but the painted backdrop inspired by the Pyrex wouldn't make sense now, which meant repainting the backdrop and starting from scratch.

Among the more common and less useful items I'd acquired in my years of buying out estates were broken umbrellas. People tended to have a difficult time letting go of them even when damaged frames made it impossible for the items to serve their purpose. Instead of tossing the lot of them into a dumpster, I'd relegated them to a bin in the corner of my storage space.

It didn't rain often in Dallas, but when it did, it rained non-stop for days straight. And when the rain ended, vibrant shades of fresh blooms contrasted nicely against bright green lawns. It would be easy enough to repaint my backdrop in slashes of blue to mimic the rain, and I could suspend the broken umbrellas to best showcase their bright patterns. I'd have Jimmy fit a patch of artificial grass into the floor of the window like a yard and add a collection of ceramic containers to hold even more umbrellas in their closed state. I even had a closetful of rain boots in assorted sizes, which I could line up along the back wall. It would be an easy display to set up, and, while it didn't show off high ticket items like the Pyrex-inspired windows had done, it would be cheerful —and far better than the black curtain that currently hung in place.

I arranged for my friend and former client Connie Duncan to join me at Nasty's cookout. Connie, in a spontaneous act of empowerment after her divorce was final, bought out a flower shop. Her experience lay more in her willingness to schlep around potted plants and chat up customers than in anything floral. In terms of friends to bring with me to the party tonight, Connie had two things going for her. She could answer my questions about flowers, and she'd probably kill to see how Nasty lived.

I went next door and hand-selected two dozen umbrellas each showing off floral patterns, stacked them in a box, and set it on my porch and checked on Tex, who was dozing on the sofa. I tiptoed out of the house and waited outside.

Connie and Effie arrived within minutes of each other. Both women wore versions of the same T-shirt: Connie's said MY LIFE MY RULES, and Effie's said SQUAD LIFE. They shared a moment of mutual appreciation for their style choices, which they celebrated with a fist bump. Then Effie turned her attention back to me.

"Captain Allen isn't his regular self," I said. It had taken the excuse of walking Rocky to get away from Tex long enough to explain the situation to Effie. "I told him I needed you to work on the inventory next door. Tell him you need his help, but don't ask him to do much."

I gave her my spare keys and called out goodbye to Rocky. Tex, having woken, opened the door. His hair stood up on one side and he blinked away sleep. I blew him a kiss. The guards changed, and I carried my box of umbrellas to Connie's new white Miata. She got out of her car.

"We need to stop at my studio first. Do you mind driving?" I asked.

"Sure. Is that box dirty? Don't you dare put it on my back seats." She popped the trunk and I set the box inside.

"You never want me to drive. What's wrong with your car?"

I stepped out into the street and pointed at the mound of dirt. She followed me and raised her eyebrows.

"You wouldn't be able to tell me anything about the dirt, would you?"

"Sure," she said. "For starters, it's about fifty feet from your garden."

"Ha ha. Seriously, though, you own a flower shop. Can you look at it and tell me anything? Is it potting soil or something else?"

"Ooh! You want me to do some forensic gardening. Hold on." She walked over to the dirt. She stooped and stuck her hand into it, and then raised her hand and sniffed it. She let the dirt fall through her fingers. "It's not potting soil. Too dry."

"Any guesses on where it came from?"

She ran her thumb and fingers against each other, then clapped a few times and then brushed her hands against each other. A reddish-brown shade clung to her palms.

"Seems like good old-fashioned Texas soil. Dirt and clay. Where'd it come from?"

"A couple of men drove up and dumped it from the back of their van."

"That's a lot of dirt," she said. "What kind of van was it? Did it have a logo?"

"Plain white van."

"Nothing good happens in the back of a plain white van," Connie said.

"True, that."

Connie volunteered to drive, the novelty of her new car not having worn off yet, and I agreed. While we weren't in a hurry, she darting in and out of traffic. Sometimes I felt

Connie fancied herself a female Mario Andretti navigating the Dallas highways, which was why I rarely asked her to drive.

We arrived at my showroom about fifteen minutes later. The black curtain still hung in my windows with the "Display in Progress" sign pinned to the center, lending a somber air to my most valuable advertising asset. The space was otherwise empty, save for the pink and white painted backdrop. On occasion, I decorated a window without the black curtain so people could watch me work, and with my windows having been covered all day, that seemed a smart choice. I took down the black curtain and draped it over the coconut chairs, then removed the portable wall and propped it alongside of an interior wall. I showed Connie my sketch and explained the concept. Her response was unexpected.

"What would it take to install this at my flower shop?"

I shrugged. "I'd have to price out the materials and time, but it's a relatively easy display to assemble." I named a price that would cover the materials and time to install it, factoring in the friends-of-the-owner discount Connie enjoyed from time to time.

"I'll take it."

I laughed. "Fine. I'll call you when the windows come down."

"No," she said. "I want it now. I just started stocking these new colorful watering cans, and this would make a perfect backdrop for them."

"I don't think people use watering cans when it rains."

"Yes, but it doesn't rain with any regularity. This reminds people that watering cans replace rain." She pulled out her corporate credit card and held it toward me. "I know you're

138

busy with this whole Tex and Lily thing, but can you install it by the weekend?"

"On one condition. You help me put the curtain back in place."

By the time Connie and I reinstalled the curtain and moved the umbrellas, stands, and rainboots to her trunk, it was after six. I wasn't going to complain about having sold two window displays in the span of a day, but my to-do list felt like the Hokey Pokey. One display in, one display out.

I entered Nasty's address into Connie's GPS and she headed toward Mockingbird Lane. Without the distraction of the shop windows, I remembered our earlier conversation about the dirt. "Why did you ask about the van that delivered the dirt?" I asked when she slowed for a construction zone.

Connie honked her horn and then flashed a smile at the construction crew. She turned to me. "That much dirt weighs about five tons. It exceeds the normal load for a residential van, so your van must have been registered for commercial use."

"And that means it's linked back to someone's business," I finished.

"Right. But businesses put their logos on their delivery vehicles. It's the cheapest form of advertising, especially if your business has to do with delivering something. So them not having a logo says more than if they did."

Two years ago, my studio had been broken into. It was one incident in a string of sabotage that kept Mad for Mod on the brink of collapse. When the insurance payment came to me, I could have cashed out and tried something new, but I hadn't wanted to do something new. I'd wanted to double down on my business and make it more successful than ever.

Shortly thereafter, I went to business school, wrote a plan for expansion, and bought the building next to my house. I'd been in too many unsavory situations to blindly assume everything would be fine this time, and among the first things I did after turning over a sizeable check and collecting the keys was install an external camera.

Time for another call to Tex.

CHAPTER SIXTEEN

I BENT DOWN AND GOT MY CELL OUT OF MY HANDBAG, AND Connie found the gas pedal and accelerated. The sudden increase in speed pushed me back against my seat. I glanced at her. "Are you trying to kill me?"

"Tex is out of the picture. I thought you might need some excitement in your life."

"He's not out of the picture," I said. Then I considered the situation. "He's out of the frame."

I called Tex, and he answered before the first ring ended.

"It's me. Where are you?" I asked.

"Your living room sofa. Don't worry, my babysitter is keeping an eye on me."

"Has she given you your evening meds yet?"

"No. Why?"

"Okay, good. Listen carefully. There's something I didn't tell you, and it might be relevant."

"Go."

I briefed him on what I remembered about the

threatening men with the truck full of dirt. "They pulled up and said they had a delivery for Lily, and then they dumped a truckload of dirt onto my car."

"Your car?"

"Technically, it was just the hood. Lily was driving my car. They didn't seem to know it was mine, not hers."

"Did you get a company name from the van?"

"No. One of the men had a delivery form on a clipboard. He tore off the top layer then crumbled it up and tossed it onto the dirt. It was an invoice from the Lakewood Arboretum, but there was nothing else on the sheet except for a big X that I watched him draw when Lily refused to sign."

"Did you get names for these guys?"

"No, but I may have gotten something better. I'm pretty sure the whole thing was picked up by the surveillance feed outside my satellite office." I waited for Tex to reply, but the phone went silent. "Hello? Did you hear me? Are you still there? You didn't pass out, did you?"

"Eighty percent of the businesses in Lakewood have inoperable security cameras aimed at their parking lots. Lily told me once when her firm investigates insurance claims, if the accident didn't take place within range of a traffic light or a bank, they can't confirm what happened, and they end up paying out."

"I'm in the twenty percent who almost lost everything once and haven't been in the mood to risk it all again. Besides, it would be an insult to the police captain in my life if I didn't take practical measures to protect myself and my company."

"Maybe I should have my detectives date business owners. Might have a positive impact on crime reduction."

"Don't make any big decisions while you're under the influence of painkillers," I said. "But if you and Effie are up to it, you might want to go next door and check the camera feed. The camera is mounted on the front entrance and has a range that goes out to the street."

"Thanks for the tip, Night."

We disconnected. Connie slowed considerably and checked the GPS unit. She looked up at a house that was situated about a block away from the street.

"This is Nasty's house?" Connie asked.

I double-checked the address from my text messages. "Yep."

Connie whistled.

It didn't surprise me to learn that Nasty lived in Highland Park. The neighborhood was among the more exclusive ones in Dallas, filled with distinctive houses positioned on larger plots than you found in the trendier parts of the city's tax base. The driveway circled around in a giant U-shape. Cars were parked on the plot of grass in the center of the U, an unusual choice for Dallas, where a green lawn was a sign of prosperity. Leave it to Nasty to buck tradition even in her home life.

Connie pulled onto the drive and circled around to the next available space. While we marveled at the house that Big Bro built, a small, scrappy puppy charged around the side of the house with a baseball in his teeth. Two boys charged after him: Adam and Gabe. They didn't seem to notice us.

"Watch out for those two," I told Connie. "They're lethal."

"They're boys. How much damage can they do?"

"Ask Tex the next time you see him."

I led Connie to the front door, which was open. I rang the bell, and a voice came over an intercom.

"Come on in, Madison."

"You don't have to ask me twice," Connie said. She opened the door and entered, and I followed. I didn't know what to expect of Nasty's house, but upon entering it, I knew it couldn't have been anything other than what it was.

The interior was white: walls, floor-to-ceiling curtains, and sofa. A white fur throw blanket had been tossed on top of a black leather ottoman. Bunches of white roses filled vases that sat on black-and-white marble end tables. The far wall was black wood from floor to ceiling, encasing a fireplace. Large green Monstera plants, well over seven feet tall, filled the space on either side of the fireplace, providing the only color in the room.

Connie whistled. "You don't think she decorated the place herself, do you?" she asked.

Before I could answer, the back door slid open and Nasty entered. I'd become used to seeing her in a tank top, tight-fitting jeans, and stilettos, but today she wore a red bikini top with cut-off jean shorts and bare feet. Her son, Huxley, followed her inside. Huxley was somewhere around two years old. He was the son of one of Dallas's wealthiest men, who was only as much a part of Nasty's life as she allowed, which was turning out to be not very much.

"The party's outside," Nasty said. "You can put your bags in my office." I could tell from the expression on Connie's face that she wanted little more than to go check out Nasty's office (and probably peek inside a couple of other rooms on the way), so I handed her my vintage handbag. She took off.

"Daisy," Huxley said, pointing at me.

"No, I'm Madison," I corrected.

"He's pointing at your pin," Nasty said.

I glanced down at my outfit and touched the metal daisy pin on my sweater. Then I looked back up. "He can identify flowers?"

"No. He thinks all flowers are daisies." She turned toward the Monstera plants next to the fireplace. "What are those, Huxley?"

"Daisies!" He looked up at her with unbridled joy, expecting to be rewarded for his genius.

She smoothed his hair away from his forehead and then kissed it and turned back to us. "Work in progress."

Nasty didn't often show this softer side to the world, and it was nice to know the few times we had gotten on the other side of our early antagonistic relationship wasn't for naught. He appeared to be more than satisfied with this solution.

Huxley plopped down on the floor by the black leather ottoman. He pulled a bin of blocks out from behind the ottoman, dumped them, and started stacking them. He said, "Daisy, daisy, daisy? Daisy!"

"Of all the words he could have picked, he went with your logo." She shook her head. "Karma."

"I thought you'd freed yourself from concerns about Karma."

"Nobody's free from Karma. I just don't believe it's the immediate cause and effect that most people do."

"Cut someone off in traffic in the morning and get a parking ticket that afternoon."

"Right. Unrelated choices that sometimes result in undesirable outcomes."

"It's always about choices with you, isn't it?"

"You're the architect of your life, Madison. We all are. Anybody who wants to blame the world for their problems isn't really interested in improving their experience."

On the floor, Huxley knocked over his tower of blocks. The outcome was undesirable, made clear by the beet red shade his face turned before he started to cry. For a little fellow, he had big lungs, and the howl he released when he took a breath probably caught the attention of the next-door neighbors.

Nasty stooped down and addressed him. "It's okay," she said. "When the blocks fall down, that means you have a chance to rebuild them. You can build a stronger foundation, and the next time, they'll be more stable." She picked up one of the blocks that had scattered close to the toes of my sneakers and handed it to him.

Huxley took the block and said, "Fall down, pick up."

"Life lesson?" I asked.

"Building blocks aren't just colorful cubes."

It was impossible to have a conversation with Nasty and not come away with a shifted perspective. In the years I'd known her, she went from being a uniformed cop on the Lakewood PD payroll to a new business owner to a respected member of the local community. That we were conversing about building blocks inside her million-dollar-plus house in Highland Park was all the evidence I needed to see that Nasty's choices had served her well.

"Is Lily out back?" I asked.

"Yes, she's by the pool." She bent down and picked up Huxley, holding him in the air for a moment before settling him on her hip. "Help yourself to whatever you want. I'll be out shortly."

Until then, it hadn't occurred to me that Nasty's baby did such banal things. We went in opposite directions. I grabbed a bottle of sparkling water and carried it to the picnic table out back. It felt good to sit outside in the transitional April air, a slight breeze disrupting the already-warm temperatures. Sunlight fell on the patio in patches, interrupted only by trees. Often, Dallas felt like a concrete jungle, but this part had been developed over a century ago, and the residents knew not to undo what their predecessors had started. It was just one element that contributed to the feeling of exclusivity.

I scanned the backyard. It was no surprise that Nasty had more land than most of the residential properties in Dallas. An in-ground pool, shaped like a kidney, was to the right just beyond a patio with not one but two picnic tables. The left side of the property was landscaped with trees, flowers, and ground cover all of which defined her property line and displayed a cacophony of colors.

Wojo nipped at Adam's heels while he played catch with a man I hadn't yet met. He was over six feet tall and had a slender face with a pointed nose. Adam tossed the ball beyond the man's reach and it landed and rolled to my feet. I scooped it up and pitched it back to Adam, who caught it. He stepped back a few feet from the impact. I pulled on a catcher's mitt that someone had left sitting on one of the picnic tables and Adam pitched the ball back to me. I caught it easily and kept the game going by pitching it to the man. Instead of keeping the three-person game of catch going, he ground the ball into his mitt and grinned at me.

"Looks like I have some competition," he said.

"No competition. I'm here for the burgers." I winked at Adam. I pulled the mitt off and set it back on the table, then made my way to the grill. David tended to the meat while I pulled a fresh bun out of the package and added a squirt of mustard. He transferred a burger to my bun and I carried my plate to the picnic table. Adam took the ball from the man and tossed it to Wojo, who ran after it and strained his jaw while retrieving it.

The man pulled a bottle of water and a bottle of beer out of a cooler and carried them to my table. He held them both out, and I took the water.

"The boys seem to know you, so you must be one of Lily's friends," he said.

"I could say the same thing about you."

"Fair enough," he said. "I'm Franklin."

"The principal?"

He seemed surprised by my recognition of his name. "I wasn't aware prep school principals had name recognition."

I chuckled. "You were right when you guessed I was friends with Lily. I'm Madison."

Franklin sat opposite me at the table and placed the unopened beer in front of him. His eyes were on the bottle of water he'd handed me, and I got the feeling he'd expected me to take the beer like the rest of the adults.

I took a sip from the water and recapped it. "Did Lily invite you?"

"No. David did. He wasn't thrilled about the party, but he thought we could get some pitching practice in."

He glanced over his shoulder at David and I followed his gaze. David had taken up the position of throwing and catching the ball with Adam. "He's going to be a real asset to our baseball team once he officially becomes a student."

"Speaking of that," I said, "I've been meaning to drop off the boys' transcripts."

He waved his hand. "Minor detail. I already told Lily I'd hold space for each of them. I just need the transcripts to make sure they're placed on the most effective academic track."

I was trying to figure out how to effectively steer the conversation from Lily's boys to Jimmy's suspension when Gabe walked up to our table. "Are you going to eat that?" he asked, pointing at my burger.

"Yes, I am," I said. "Didn't you already have two?"

"I gave one to my brother."

"I can make you another if you're still hungry." I stood and addressed Franklin. "Would you like one too?" I asked him.

He checked his watch. "No, I'm not going to stay for long. I just dropped by to help welcome the boys to Dallas." He stood. "I'm going inside to make my apologies." He left.

I carried my burger to the grill. The tray of cooked burgers was empty, so I cooked up four more, I hadn't realized just how hungry I was, so I made mine a double with one of the new patties and carried my plate to the table. I finished everything but the bun.

Gabe didn't bother to sit. He ate his burger in about three bites, washed it down with a swig from a can of soda, and set the can on a table. David had gone inside, so Gabe picked up the catcher's mitt left behind and tossed the ball to Adam.

I closed my eyes and tipped my head back, letting the remaining streaks of sun warm my face. The scent of mesquite filled the air, mingling with waxy tiki torches burning to keep bugs away, burgers and hot dogs coming off the grill, and chopped onions and mustard. The soundtrack fit the perfect April day: the boys laughing, bottles clinking, Wojo barking, Huxley trying out new words, and doors opening and closing.

"Who are they?" I heard Gabe ask.

I opened my eyes. Even though I wore sunglasses, it took a moment to adjust to the bright sunlight. Detective Sue Niedermeier and her partner, Jerry, stood talking to Nasty. Adam and George, the ten- and fifteen-year-olds of Lily's brood, sat at the patio table behind her. Adam's plate held a hamburger and a hot dog. George gazed lovingly at Nasty from a distance.

Something about the scene felt off. Would Nasty have invited the two detectives investigating the case of Lily's husband to a cookout at her house? That didn't seem likely. In fact, Nasty didn't look like she'd expected the detectives to show up on her doorstep at all. She certainly wasn't playing the role of hostess.

"Where's your mom?" I asked Gabe.

"She went inside."

I lowered my voice. "Go in and stay with her." I didn't tell him why I'd asked: that I thought it best that Tex's sister avoid a run-in with the homicide detectives investigating his father's murder. Gabe wandered away, and I stood up and dusted the crumbs from my dress, preparing to nose my way into things.

I walked up to the detectives. "Hi, Sue, Jerry," I said cheerfully.

Sue glanced at me and pressed her lips together, giving

the sort of nonsmile you give someone when a smile might be expected but more pressing issues override the moment. She kept her voice low, but I was too close not to hear what she said.

"I'm sorry. I know this is inconvenient, but we need you to come with us."

"What's going on?" I asked. "Does this have to do with Gil Banks?"

"Stay out of this, Madison," Nasty said. "Don't say another word."

Sue kept her eyes on Nasty. "Do you have someone to watch Huxley?"

I stared at Nasty and then at Sue and Jerry and back at Sue. Something about the moment didn't add up. I'd sent Gabe inside to keep Lily out of the picture, but it was starting to seem as though they weren't here for her.

"Detective?" I prompted.

"Let's go," Jerry said. He reached out toward Nasty and Sue put her hand on his arm and kept him from contacting Nasty.

"She has a house full of company," I told Sue. "What's so important that it can't wait until later?"

But Sue didn't answer me. Nasty did. "Madison, I need you to stay here."

"Where are you going?"

"We're taking her to the police station," Jerry said. "Ms. Nast is being detained for the murder of Gil Banks."

CHAPTER SEVENTEEN

I SHIFTED MY ATTENTION FROM THE DETECTIVES TO NASTY. She was staring directly back at me. She still carried herself with confidence, but her eyes had gone flat. For the first time since I'd met her, I saw something other than extreme self-assuredness. I saw despair.

"Does Captain Allen know you're here?" I asked Sue.

It was Jerry who answered. "We haven't been able to reach him," he said. "I called my old captain and spelled out the evidence we have and he said to bring her in and that we can catch Captain Allen up tomorrow."

I couldn't help but see an apology in Sue's face. "Do you know where Captain Allen is?" she asked.

"He could be any number of places," I said, which felt close enough to the truth to keep me from feeling like I was lying to the cops. I scanned the three faces in front of me, making sure to hold eye contact with Nasty for a moment longer than with the others. "I'll take care of..." I trailed off, not knowing which pending problem of Nasty's I should spearhead first. "Huxley." The responsibility for a two-year-old was just one of the looming problems I wasn't sure I was equipped to solve.

Nasty was enough of a friend to the police to keep them from making a scene while they escorted her off her property, but the fact that they'd shown up here, during her cookout, to detain her at the police station, was alarming. Nasty? What evidence could they possibly have found to make them turn on her?

I watched the three of them enter the house. Adam was almost done with his burger. George stared at the door through which the detectives had led Nasty. His mouth turned down. Once again, young love had been thwarted, but this time, it was worse than before.

"Where's your mother?" I called out to the boys.

"She went to the bathroom," Adam said. He'd finished his burger and was already two bites into his hot dog. A smear of mustard clung to the right side of his mouth. "Where'd those two people take your girlfriend?" he asked George before swallowing his food.

George glanced at me. When he caught me watching him, his face turned beet red. He stood up and left Adam sitting alone on the bench. Lily was on her way out the back door, and she blocked his entrance.

"Have you had enough to eat?" she asked brightly.

"I'm not hungry." George shouldered his way past Lily and went into the house.

"Hormones," Lily, shaking her head.

In the absence of Nasty, the party atmosphere felt inappropriate. The last of the sunlight had disappeared, and the formerly festive backyard now felt unsettling. A quick mental inventory left me overwhelmed with the reality of three adult women and five boys between the ages of toddler and seventeen. I'd already seen the damage four of those five boys could do to Tex, and I feared the long-term damage of leaving Nasty's baby in their company.

Lily held a bottle of Lone Star beer. "Where's Donna?" she asked.

I stared back at Lily. She didn't know what had happened. She'd been inside the house when the cops arrived, and they'd made short shrift of their business. I glanced over my shoulder and checked to see who could hear me. Adam was getting a third hot dog from the grill, and Wojo, having determined Adam was his best source for food, circled the boy's ankles. Adam pinched a piece of burger off a cooked patty that sat on a plate and looked around to see who was watching. He froze when he saw me. I smiled, and he turned his attention back to Wojo and handed him the piece of burger.

"We have a problem," I said in a low voice. "The detectives who are investigating Gil's murder just detained Na —Donna."

"They arrested her?" Lily asked.

"It wasn't an arrest. They took her to the precinct for questioning."

"That's preliminary to an arrest. If they had follow-up questions for her, they would have talked to her here. This house has ample space to offer them privacy even with all of us here."

Lily was right, and I knew it, mainly because of Tex. That was probably how Lily knew it too. What she and Tex knew about each other's lives interested me, especially since Tex had said they'd grown apart.

"I'm sure it's nothing," I said. "She serviced a security contract at the arboretum. They may have picked up her DNA at the scene, and they need her to explain that."

"Donna may have had a contract with Gil and Ed, but she wouldn't have serviced the contract herself. She's got a team of full-time field reps to do that."

I'd questioned that, too, until Nasty told me the truth: this wasn't the first break-in at one of her businesses, and the negative press had hurt business. She'd had to let go of a portion of her field team.

Nasty was a hands-off businesswoman. She had created her company and recruited aggressively. Now she sat on the board of directors of a handful of Dallas-area businesses and had a say in city business. She could run for mayor and probably win, but I didn't think she wanted the hassle of politics. Nasty lived by a code: what was best for her. So why had she broken her own rules to take on the inconvenience of tending to Gil Banks's bad habits? I was starting to think Nasty had something to hide, something none of us knew.

I set Huxley on a rocking chair and sat across from Lily. "I talked to Detective Niedermeier earlier today, and she didn't say anything about Nasty."

"When was that?"

"After I talked to you. I called her about the calendar. She came out to the house."

"She didn't take it, did she?"

"The calendar? No. Why?"

"The house belongs to me. She'd need my permission to take it, and she didn't contact me."

"Right." Sue had said as much. I still remembered her exact words: *not yours to give.* At the time, I'd felt as if she were being extra-cautious because she suspected Lily of something and wanted to be sure to follow procedure and leave none of her actions up to misinterpretation. What had she discovered between this afternoon and today that pointed her in Nasty's direction instead?

I hadn't given Sue the calendar, but I *had* given her the vial of dirt. She'd said she was sending it to the lab. I already knew real life wasn't like the cop shows on TV. It would be weeks before she had a report on the contents of that dirt. I glanced up at Nasty's freshly landscaped backyard. It was the thinnest of connections. There had to be something more, but still, I regretted telling Sue about it before I'd had a chance to talk to Tex.

I glanced at Huxley, who had somehow gotten out of the chair and was on his way across the room. I stood up and scooped him up, then sat in the rocking chair with him on my lap. The last thing we needed was for Huxley to make a break for it.

"I found something in my spare bedroom. Something I'm going to need you to explain."

Lily stopped rocking. She fell quiet, waiting for me to continue.

"It was a five million dollar life insurance policy and a set of divorce papers. Gil left a note on them that made it seem like he hadn't changed his mind like you said. What am I missing?"

The question didn't appear to come as a surprise to Lily. "Gil was a rat. He was always a rat. I served him with divorce papers half a dozen times over the past year. He was bleeding me dry with legal fees and he knew it. I finally fired my lawyer and printed up my own papers from a Zoom Legal template."

"What happened?"

"He died."

"Before that. What made him change his mind?"

Lily looked down at her hands. "He didn't."

"What?"

This time, she looked at me. "Gil didn't change his mind. He was never going to change his mind. I couldn't take it anymore, so I told him I was moving to Dallas. I said if he wanted a wife and kids so badly that he wouldn't divorce us, then he would have to provide for us. Starting with a house."

"The house on Cinderella Lane."

Lily nodded. "I don't think he expected me to actually pack up everything we owned and sell the house in Austin. But I was exhausted, Madison. I'd been fighting with that man for too long. I thought I could force his hand. He must have had a life here in Dallas, a life we weren't a part of. And me showing up with a ready-made family would be a threat to that."

"And the insurance policy?"

She glanced over both of her shoulders to make sure no one else was within earshot. "I tried to back him into a corner. I drew up the policy myself and told him he was going to sign one document or the other. And not twenty-four hours later he had an international job offer and he gave me the house. He told me he signed his copy of the divorce agreement and left it for me at his lab, but you know how that went. I don't know if our arrival had anything to do with what happened at the arboretum, but I'm not sorry he's dead," she said.

Until now, I'd thought Lily's arrival was what she'd said: triggered by Gil's agreement to divorce. But if that had never happened, then she was right. Her arrival may have set the wheels of Gil's demise into motion. Now more than ever, it seemed important to understand what his life was like before she showed up, and the only clue I had about that was his calendar.

"What day is it?" I asked.

"Wednesday."

"Wait here." I transferred Huxley to her arms and he wriggled free and stumbled a few feet away and picked up his plush rocket. "Keep an eye on everybody. I'll be right back."

Buzzing with anticipation, I went inside the house. I found Connie stirring something on the induction stovetop.

"Where's Nasty's office?" I asked her.

"Huh?"

"Her office. She told you to put our handbags inside it."

"It's the second door on the right. Why? Are we leaving already?"

I stared at her. "Do you know what happened outside?"

"I can't take it out there. I went vegan two months ago, and the scent of burgers was making me crazy. Nasty told me to raid her pantry. I'm making quinoa."

"Don't go anywhere," I said. "I'll be right back."

I followed Connie's directions to Nasty's office. The rest of her house was a study in black and white, but her office was red. The shock of entering it was like doing an espresso shot, boosting my already coursing adrenaline. I walked to her desk, a white quartz table with brushed gold legs that held a desk lamp and a vase of flowers, and sat in her white ergonomic leather chair. I opened and closed several drawers, searching for a calendar, all the while knowing my actions were futile. Nasty wouldn't use a paper calendar. Those were for people like me, nostalgia freaks who liked the feeling of a pen and paper, who got pleasure from seeing our month-at-a-glance and didn't mind the scribbles in the margins when our plans changed.

Nasty would keep her schedule on her computer, and I knew one person who could potentially get me access.

I called Effie.

"Hey, boss," she answered. "You want to talk to Captain Allen?"

"Is he there?"

"He's in the back. Hang on. I'll get him."

"No, Effie, I need to talk to you. Can you get me into Nasty's computer?"

Effie didn't say anything at first. Then she said, "Um, boss? I think that might be a violation of her privacy."

"Nasty's in trouble," I said, not mincing words. "The police just took her to the station for detention. I'm trying to help, but I can't blindly help her if it puts Captain Allen's sister at risk. I was hoping to see where Nasty has been in the past couple of weeks, maybe find out if her path overlapped with Gil Banks—"

"I don't need to get you into her computer to answer that," Effie said. "It did. At speed dating."

CHAPTER EIGHTEEN

I felt the way I'd felt in the car with Connie when she slammed on the brakes. "Nasty goes to speed dating?"

"Yep."

"Do you know where this speed dating is?"

"That upscale taco restaurant on Greenville Avenue. It's not far from your studio."

"And it's every Wednesday?"

"Yes. Seven to nine. She must have skipped tonight because Lily was in town."

I glanced at the clock. It was ten after eight. "Thanks, Effie." I was about to hang up when I remembered Tex. "Don't tell Captain Allen I called, okay?"

"Sure, boss. I'll keep him busy."

It wasn't so much that I wanted to keep information from Tex—in fact, the opposite was true. But the situation was getting complicated. Sue and Jerry needed to talk to Tex because he was their captain. They didn't know where he was, and that might work for us. But Nasty was not only his friend. She was one of them—or had been when she worked on the force. And Nasty's involvement complicated matters as far as Lily was concerned.

I also wasn't sure I wanted to talk to Tex about everything that had happened, because I couldn't help thinking Lily was still hiding something. The way she kicked Gil's body at the arboretum. The divorce papers she had hidden in her luggage. The dismissive way she talked about his murder. And before all that, the way she'd left my house unexpectedly the morning Gil was murdered.

I understood that she'd been under his thumb for a decade, but anybody would have felt an emotional shift when he died. Just thinking of the energy it had taken for her to battle Gil for all those years and then learning it was over, just like that, would have demanded a release. But Lily hadn't acted like someone whose life had changed. She just kept on keeping on. I wanted to like her, to trust her, to feel a sisterly bond with her, but I couldn't shake the feeling that she knew something about Gil she wasn't telling any of us.

Plus, if Lily had been involved in her husband's murder, Nasty's detainment was a convenient piece of misdirection.

I shook the thought from my mind. That kind of accusation would drive an irreparable wedge between Tex and me. I knew what Tex and I had was special, but I wasn't willing to put it up against that familial bond. I wasn't willing to risk losing everything if the chips didn't fall my way.

When I returned to the living area, I found Connie and Huxley on the sofa. Huxley was attempting to explain some important concept to Connie, who was doing her best to pretend she understood. He held a stuffed rocket toward her and said, "Moo."

"No. It's a rocket," she said. "It goes to outer space."

Huxley pointed at the rocket. "Moo. Moo."

"Cows go moo. Rockets go..." She looked up at me. "What noise do rockets make?"

"Moo! Moo!" Huxley said. He climbed down from the ottoman and retrieved a plush crescent moon from his bin of toys. "Moo!"

Connie took the toy. "He's been saying 'moon.'" She stared at him then looked at me. "You don't think he actually understands the concept of space travel, do you?"

"I don't think he's talking about cows." I smiled gently at Huxley, who appeared to be frustrated by Connie's lack of understanding. I took the rocket from Connie's hand and gave it back to Huxley. "Moon," I said.

"Made of cheese," he said back.

We weren't quite at Mensa level yet.

I went to the sliding glass door and stared outside. Lily and George sat at the table, each of them on their phones. Gabe and Adam were on opposite sides of the yard, each wearing a catcher's mitt, pitching and catching a baseball. I didn't know where David had gone, but taking inventory of the four boys was the last thing on my mind.

"We have a problem," I told Connie in a low voice. "Nasty's in trouble, and I can't tell Tex because it ties back to his sister. Can you stay here with her and the kids while I go check something out?"

"Is that smart?"

"I don't think they're a family of Dexters, but I'm not comfortable leaving Huxley here."

"Not me. You. I'm not comfortable letting you go off to some secret meeting."

"It's not a secret meeting. It's speed dating." I checked my watch. "It ends in half an hour."

"The one at the taco restaurant on Greenville?"

"Yes. How'd you know?"

"It's Wednesday."

"Have you been there?"

"Sure," Connie said. "Just because I was married to a philandering idiot doesn't mean I gave up on finding love."

"Have you ever seen Nasty there?"

"No, but she wouldn't be there when I was."

"Why not?"

"Age groups. She's twenty-nine, right?"

"She might be thirty by now."

"Still, I'm in the forty-plus group. We're Wednesdays. She's Thursdays."

"That doesn't make sense. Effie said Nasty went every Wednesday."

"Maybe she waits in the parking lot to check out the older candidates."

I was only half paying attention to Connie. My mind raced to fill holes, holes that felt far from questions about botany and plant research.

"New plan," I said. "Find Huxley's diaper bag. You're both coming with me."

Connie, Huxley, and I arrived at the taco restaurant about fifteen minutes after leaving Nasty's house. Most of the parking spaces were full, indicating the event was popular. The restaurant was a curious place to host a singles mixer, considering the ingredients found in most Mexican food, but this was Dallas, and if you didn't like Tex-Mex, you were probably not looking to meet up with someone who did.

"What's your plan?" Connie asked. Huxley stood on Connie's thighs, and she held his fists in her palms.

I shrugged. "I suppose I'll go in and talk to the organizers. Maybe if I tell them Gil was murdered, they'll turn over their roster and cooperate."

"With who—you?" She laughed. "No offense, Mad, but you're dressed like a golfer with a metal daisy pinned to your sweater. You don't exactly look official."

"Right. But we know Gil came here every Wednesday, and now we know Nasty came here too. There's something going down here. What would Nasty do?"

I stared at the restaurant's doors. It was eight thirty-eight, and if we waited out here, everyone inside would eventually come out. But what would that tell us? Nothing.

Everything Connie said was right, and this was no time to quibble about matters like personal style choices.

"Trade clothes with me," I said.

"What?"

"You're right about my outfit. There's no time for me to hit the mall and find something more suitable."

It would have been nice to have tinted windows, but this was not the time to be concerned with that either. Connie moved Huxley to the back seat and then pulled her MY LIFE MY RULES T-shirt over her head while I removed my vintage golf outfit. We traded garments, and I pulled on her low-rise jeans. How did women wear these? How did they sit down in restaurants and not show off their underpants?

"Wait here with Huxley. If anything happens, don't worry about me. I'll find a way home."

"Mad, this is speed dating. If you ask someone for a ride home, they might think it's their lucky night."

"I am so glad I'm in a relationship," I said and closed the door before I could hear her reply.

I approached the entrance to the restaurant. The lot was full, but I'd seen no one leave. I didn't know how these events worked, and if not for Huxley's presence, I might have invited Connie along, since she knew the lay of the land.

I'd eaten at this restaurant previously but felt it had been too much of a scene. They had both indoor and outdoor seating, and the walls were made of thick glass to minimize the barrier between both. As I reached for the door handle, I saw a familiar-looking woman striding toward me. She had long copper-and-brown-streaked hair, dark plum lipstick, and a wrap dress that showed off her curves. It was Nasty.

Except it wasn't.

I felt a chill sweep through me, which could have been courtesy of the restaurant's extreme air-conditioning, but it felt like something more. If the police had enough evidence to implicate Nasty in Gil's murder, then they had something more than I did. And the last information I'd given them was Gil's datebook. I chewed my peeling lips and produced a timeline for tonight. While I was partying at Nasty's house, speed dating had started. Sue and Jerry could have come here to check things out, and with their very official badges, they might have even gotten information.

I pulled the heavy glass door open and watched the woman enter the ladies' room. From the back view of her, I'd swear she was Nasty. As I forgot about my original goal and headed toward her, a restaurant employee who'd been bent over behind the hostess stand straightened up and acknowledged me.

"Hi," he said. "How many in your party?"

I waved my hand to shoo him off. "I'm not here to eat. I'm here for speed dating."

"You're late," he said. He glanced at his phone, which sat on the hostess stand. "There's only about twenty minutes left."

"Right," I said. "I meant I'm here to meet a friend who's at speed dating. I'm her ride home."

"Then you're early. There's still twenty minutes left."

"Right." I looked past him. "Would it be possible for me to use the restroom?" I asked.

"Restroom is for paying customers only," he said, and just as I was about to write him off as a pain in my tush, he added in a conspiratorial voice, "You can order a Coke at the bar for a dollar."

I thanked him and went to the bar. I ordered a club soda, told the bartender I'd be right back, then went to the restroom. The door opened as I pulled on the handle. The woman I'd seen earlier faced me. We made eye contact, but she didn't smile or frown or act in any way as if she knew who I was. That left me more unsettled than I'd been before I stared her in the face.

I allowed her to pass me and then called to her back, "Donna?"

She stopped and turned around. "Yes?" she answered. She blinked a couple of times. "I tore a contact earlier and didn't have a spare pair, so I'm a little blind. Nice to see you again." She turned away from me.

"Wait!" I called out. I let go of the bathroom door and caught up with her. "Are you okay?"

"Sure. Why?"

"You're not acting like yourself."

From this close, I could tell this woman wasn't Nasty, but now she'd claimed to be, and that interested me more.

But before she had a chance to respond, a baby wailed from somewhere behind me. I turned and saw Connie and Huxley enter the restaurant. Connie was doing her best to use Huxley's plush rocket to distract him from his tantrum.

"Huxley?" the woman asked. She moved past me and approached Connie, who stared at her with the same bewilderment I felt. Huxley turned to see her, and she reached out for him. There was no way I would allow a Nasty impersonator to take her act this far, but Huxley's face shifted into smiles, and he called out, "Lo! Lo! Lo!" He stretched his arms out toward the woman, and as soon as she took him from Connie's arms, he hugged the woman and nuzzled his face into her chest.

"Lo?" I asked.

The woman repositioned Huxley on her hip and looked back and forth between Connie's face and mine. "You probably already know I'm not Donna. I'm her older sister, Lola."

CHAPTER NINETEEN

"Nasty has a sister?" Connie asked. "I mean, Donna Nast has a sister?" She turned to Lola. "Sorry. That was rude."

"Please. People have been calling us Nasty since grade school."

Nasty once told me the same thing—that, along with their mother, they were five nasty women. At the time, she'd said it with a sort of pride. She told me they lived in and around Dallas and saw one another on occasion.

"I'm Madison Night," I said by way of introduction. "This is Connie Duncan."

"Lola Nast," Nasty's sister said.

"Are you here for speed dating?"

"Yes. I've been seeing someone I met here last year, but he stood me up for our last two dates. I—it sounds desperate now that I think about it, but I thought if I came here, I might run into him, and he might tell me what happened."

Another puzzle piece fell into place. I glanced at Connie, but she only knew the bare minimum of the situation, and no lightbulbs had gone off over her head. The novelty of meeting Nasty's sister had been replaced by Huxley's attempt to grab the daisy pin on the sweater I'd swapped for Connie's T-shirt.

"Was the man who stood you up named Gil Banks?"

A cloud passed over Lola's face. "How did you know? Was he seeing you too? I hate when Donna's right."

"What did Donna tell you?"

"She told me to drop him. That was back when I first told her about this place and how I'd met someone. She asked his name, and I told her without thinking too much about it. I should have known she couldn't just leave well enough alone. Can you believe she ran a background check on him? She could lose her company for something like that."

That was a big risk for Nasty to take, which frightened me even more. "What did she find?"

Lola's eyebrows pulled together, and a crooked crease appeared between them. "How did you know she found something?'

"She wouldn't have warned you away if she didn't."

Lola's shoulders slumped. Her wrap dress, which she seemed to have chosen because she filled it out well, had shifted, pulling and tugging in all the wrong places. "I don't know what she found. I didn't want to know. I told her I didn't want to hear the secrets she dug up. Everybody has skeletons in their closets. Gil was a gentleman. He used to bring me flowers."

"Did he tell you what he did for a living?"

She looked at me funny, as if it were a foregone conclusion that a nice gentleman who brought her flowers would tell her what he did for a living. "He's an organic gardener. He has a nursery behind his house, and he sells vegetables at the local farmers' market."

I looked at Connie. Even with Huxley claiming her attention, she knew those claims were fiction.

"Oh, girl," Connie said. "I'm so sorry."

"About what?"

"Lola," I said, "I think we need to have a long talk."

The taco restaurant was not the best setting for an intimate discussion of Gil's murder, so we needed a Plan B. Lily and the boys were at Nasty's house. Nasty was with the police. Tex was with Effie at my place. In the grand game of musical houses, Tex's townhouse was our best chance for a private place to converse.

Even though Huxley obviously recognized Lola, I wasn't about to just hand him over to her. I suggested she ride along with us, but she didn't want to leave her car, so she climbed into her cherry red Mustang and followed Connie's Miata. I couldn't wait to change back into my own clothes, but Tex's townhouse would be a better place for that than the bathroom of the taco restaurant (or the parking lot).

Tex's place was quiet. No Tex, no TV, no boys, no dog. I led our small procession through the garage and into the kitchen. Connie, who'd never been here, opened and closed cabinets to see how Tex lived. She looked at me apologetically, and I shook my head at her behavior.

"The captain of the Lakewood Police Department has Cap'n Crunch in his pantry," she said. "That man is a mystery unto himself."

After Connie and I swapped clothes back in Tex's bedroom ("Lavender sheets?" "What does he sleep in?" "Does he actually use soap on a rope?"), we returned to the living room. Lola sat on the floor with Huxley, who was neatly stacking throw pillows into a tower.

Then Lola moved from the floor to the sofa. I sat next to her, and Connie entered the kitchen and opened a bottle of wine. She didn't ask if either one of us wanted it but rather announced her actions. I just assumed it was an excuse to go through more of Tex's cupboards.

"Why were you using Donna's name at speed dating?" I asked. "You said you've been there before, so wouldn't they know you?"

"The thing about speed dating is that you check in with your ID, but you can use a different name if you want," Lola said. "It's a privacy measure of sorts. They discovered people were doing it anyway, so they adopted it as part of their program. And I thought if Gil heard someone say 'Lola,' he'd know it was me, and he might leave before I had a chance to talk to him. So I used Donna's name instead."

"You have two other sisters. Why go with hers?"

"My other two sisters are married. I didn't want anything I did getting either of them in trouble."

"Connie said the speed dating is divided up into age groups."

"Right. Wednesday is for the thirty-five-to-forty-five crowd, and Thursdays are for twenty-five to thirty-five. They check your ID when you get there, but you print whatever name you want to go by for the night. Why all the questions? What's going on?"

I glanced into the kitchen. Connie was staring into a drawer. From the general layout of the kitchen, I figured she was looking in the drawer where Tex kept koozies. I'd never once seen him use one, but the man had a collection to rival my inventory of tasseled summer hats—something he'd mentioned when I inquired about the foam can holders. Connie would be occupied for a while. I turned back to Lola.

"I need to tell you a few things," I told her. "Some of them may be the same things Donna wanted you to know, but this time, I think you need to listen."

"Is Gil okay?"

I didn't mince words. "Gil's dead."

All color drained from Lola's face.

"Murdered. Your sister was taken to the police station earlier tonight, where she'll likely be detained for twenty-four hours. The police came to a cookout at her house. They seem to have something that links her to Gil."

"There isn't anything that links Donna to Gil," Lola said.

"Actually, there is. Gil wasn't a gardener. He was a botanist. He conducted privately funded research at the Lakewood Arboretum, and Donna serviced his security contract."

Lola's face was blank. It was uncanny, as if this woman in front of me were a deepfake, a copy of Nasty that looked and talked like her but wasn't always one step ahead of me. Her dark plum lipstick had faded in the center, leaving behind her lips' natural rosy hue. Her brows were immaculate, and her makeup was subtle but flattering. Her hair was shaded in the same tones as Nasty's—highlights in copper, lowlights in deep, mahogany brown, and a rich mid-range of coffee. I wondered if all the Nasty women had this same hairstyle, and if so, did they get a group discount?

It seemed clear that everything I'd told Lola was new information, and there was more where that came from. But the bigger issue was Nasty being taken away from her house, and that—that one thing—felt like it went back to speed dating.

"Earlier today, I found a calendar at Gil's house. It had fallen under his Scandinavian étagère, and I don't think he knew he left it behind when he moved out."

"Gil didn't move," she said. "He lives in an apartment at Midway Crossing."

"No, he lives—lived—in a mid-century ranch house on Cinderella Lane."

"That's his friend's house. We went there once. He said he left something there and had to stop off. He wanted me to wait in the car, but—you know." She didn't bother playing coy. "It was a big empty house, and that felt like an opportunity to... Well, I waited until he was inside and snuck in after him. I surprised him in the bedroom."

"How long were you there?"

"In the bedroom or in the house?"

I raised my eyebrows.

"A couple of hours, I'd say. There are a lot of rooms."

I couldn't fault Lola for—well, for her bad taste in men, for starters, but my low opinion of Gil sank even further. He refused to give in to Lily's requests for a divorce, but here he'd been catting around Dallas's singles scene all the while.

"Did you know Gil was married?"

"No, he wasn't. He couldn't have been. I told you—they run a background check to make sure everyone's on the up and up. Dallas has lots of other dating events that don't care so much about those things. If he were married, he could have just gone to one of them and lied about it."

Lola seemed sure about Gil, and without Lily here to

show Lola her wedding photos, I didn't know how to convince her. But something Lola said came back to me.

"You said he went there to get something. Do you know what it was?"

"His calendar."

I tried to suppress my excitement. "Did you see it?"

"No. On the car ride away from the house, he said I made him forget all about it." Lola attempted, unsuccessfully, to hide her pride at this accusation.

I nodded but didn't say anything. I pieced together how this information fit with what I knew. Gil knew he'd left the calendar behind. He went to the house to get it, and Lola surprised him and took his mind off his worries for a few hours. They left, and the calendar remained there. And then, an undetermined number of days later, Gil gave the house to Lily as part of their divorce settlement.

"This townhouse belongs to Captain Tex Allen of the Lakewood Police Department."

"I know Tex. He used to date my sister."

"Mad dates him now," Connie chimed in from the kitchen. I turned to glare at her. She shrugged.

I turned back to Lola. "This whole thing with Gil has gotten complicated. I know things you don't, and you know things I don't. And the police think they know something I don't believe is true."

Lola pulled her long hair over one shoulder in the same gesture I'd watched Nasty make a hundred times, and she settled in on the sofa. We'd taken our eyes off Huxley for less than a minute, and he had already halfway up the stairs.

Lola stood up and approached Huxley. She picked him

up, carried him back to the sofa, and held him on her lap. Huxley's face turned red, and he let out an ear-piercing wail.

"He needs his diaper changed," Lola said. She looked at me and then Connie.

Connie set Nasty's diaper bag on Tex's kitchen counter and pulled out a fresh one and a package of wipes. Lola carried Huxley to the kitchen where she went about the business of cleaning him up.

For the next few minutes, the only sound in the townhouse was a baby crying. It made me realize how difficult Nasty's life had become, how she managed to raise him while running her empire and how it was all at risk because of her sister's actions.

Lola finished with Huxley's diaper and held him up in front of her. He stopped crying and waved his fists around. His round cheeks shone and he looked like he was smiling.

Lola carried him back over to the sofa and sat down, resting him on her thigh. "I don't know how Gil could have faked being single, but he's gone and if my sister is in trouble because of him," she paused to cover Huxley's ears, "I'll kill the bastard."

"He's already dead, remember?" Connie called out from the kitchen. She really was picking up the highlights of the conversation.

"Doesn't matter. I'll kill him again."

"Here's what I know," I said. "Gil left that house on Cinderella Lane to his wife. He was about to leave the country but turned up dead instead. I'm working on a decorating overhaul there, and I found his calendar under the étagère. That seemed significant, so I called the police."

Lola held out her hand to stop me. "The police or Tex?"

"The police."

"Why didn't you call Tex? If you two are so close—"

"He's been unavailable for a few days."

"Are you sure you're dating him?" Lola asked. She glanced at my yellow and green golf outfit. "You don't look like his type."

Now wasn't the time to defend my relationship. I stood quickly and looked down at Huxley. "Gil and his wife Lily have four boys who have sidelined Tex with a black eye, laxatives on his steak, and a swarm of bees. He's been in and out of the hospital over the past few days, and at the moment, he's resting at my house because Lily has been staying here."

Lola didn't say anything for a few seconds. I knew I'd lost my cool and was acting like an irrational woman. My relationship with Tex had never been based on jealousy and possessive behavior, and my response surprised me. I was surrounded by people who had people: families, siblings, parents, and spouses, and I felt like a consolation prize still sitting on the shelf.

Lola stood abruptly. She picked up her handbag and pulled out a set of keys attached to a rose gold fob. She worried the metal with her thumb. "Gil really had kids?" she asked. "Boys?"

"Four of them between the ages of ten and seventeen."

"They're a real menace to society," Connie called out.

There was much more I could tell Lola: about the plant research left behind for Lily, the men who'd dumped a truck load of dirt onto my car, and the fortuitous job offer out of the country. If she didn't want to believe Gil was married, though, then she might not believe anything else I had to say.

But I did have the keys to the Cinderella house, and if Lola had been there, she might know about something else.

I flexed my knee, which was swollen from all of the up and down of the day. "You said you'd been to the house on Cinderella Lane. That's where the police found the calendar, the clue that led them to your sister."

"How do you know that's what they found?"

"I told you, when I found the calendar, I called Detective Niedermeier. She came out to the house and looked at it."

"But she didn't take it?"

"She couldn't take it. She even said it wasn't mine to give."

Lola shook her head. "Then I don't get it. How could that calendar be the clue that led them to my sister?"

She had a point. Sue had very specifically refused possession of the calendar, but something about the visit to that house had led her to Nasty. Maybe the calendar wasn't the clue, but that meant Sue had seen something that I'd missed.

Something stank, and this time, it wasn't Huxley's diapers.

"Connie, how do you feel about watching Huxley for the next few hours?"

CHAPTER TWENTY

LOLA INSISTED ON DRIVING. IT WAS CLOSING IN ON TEN, AND Lily's new neighborhood was quiet. I briefly wondered how quickly her boys would rack up their first complaint from a neighbor after they moved in.

I unlocked the front door and led the way. She glanced into the living room, where Jimmy had pulled up most of the carpet, revealing rotted hardwood underneath. My heart sank at the sight, but that was always a risk when removing old carpeting, and it was one of a mounting stack of problems I would deal with tomorrow. I switched on the lights as we went farther into the house. Lola scanned the place while we advanced slowly.

"This place looks different now that it's empty," she said. "Not as sexy."

When I'd left earlier, I hadn't closed the blinds over the sliding glass doors. There was a heavy glare against the glass. I turned off the lights, slid the back door open, and stepped out onto the patio. I looked up and spotted exterior lights and then looked from side to side until I found a switch. Once I flipped it, the patio was awash in a yellow cast of light. I saw the shovels propped against the side of the potting shed and the row of aluminum cages placed to shield tomato plants from hungry critters. At a passing glance, it all looked like a typical backyard. But something was off.

A bright floodlight came on and temporarily blinded me. I heard the racking of a shotgun and an angry male voice say, "I already warned you once. This is private property."

My hands shot up in the air, and I turned toward the voice. The bright light made it impossible to see the speaker, but I recognized the voice from earlier. "Harry? It's Madison Night. I'm the decorator."

After a few terrifying seconds, he unracked his gun. "You always work this late?"

"I'm not here for work." I shielded my eyes and approached the rickety wooden fence. Harry switched off the bright lantern, and the sudden loss of light left me as blind as I'd been when the light was in my eyes. I held my hands out and felt for the fence. I closed my eyes for a second and then opened them, detecting the general shapes that I was headed toward.

Lola hadn't followed me outside. It bothered me a little bit that she was unsupervised in a house where the police had found enough evidence to detain her sister, but I couldn't be in two places at once. "I thought you told me you weren't a *Rear Window* type," I said, hoping Harry wouldn't be offended by the reference or implication.

"Too much action on this side of the fence over the past week to ignore," he said. "All that business today, that was because of you and this decorating job?"

"My team quit at five."

He frowned. "How many people are on this team of yours?"

"Two. Me and a young carpenter."

"How young?"

"High school senior."

"He cut school to work for you?"

"He was suspended for eating brownies intended for the baseball team."

Harry shook his head. "Used to be you had to do something wrong to get suspended. You sure he wasn't pulling your leg?"

"Jimmy is one of those rare individuals who compulsively tells the truth. It's refreshing." I turned around and glanced at the house, wondering what Lola was up to. "But you said someone was here after that?"

"Middle-aged blonde and a younger guy. Looked like police dicks, if you ask me. They parked out front and walked through the yard. Though it was unusual that they didn't come through the house. They walked around and took pictures of the backyard, and then they left."

I turned my back to Harry and leaned against the fence. It sagged under my weight. I stood straight and tried to see what Sue had seen. It made sense that whatever this clue was, it was outside. They didn't have permission to enter the house. I wasn't sure they were able to enter the yard, but there might be some sort of rule about interior and exterior searches. I'd have to ask Tex.

But right now, Tex was recovering from his own troubles, and I was left alone trying to look out for his sister, doing a miserable job in the process.

I turned my head to the side. "Harry, can you turn that light back on?"

"Sure." Harry switched on his floodlight, bathing the backyard in light again. Lights illuminated the windows of the house behind us, and another neighbor, silhouetted against her window, peered outside at us.

Drawing this much attention to the house was a bad idea. If Lily really were to move in here, then she'd do so with curious neighbors, some of whom might pass judgment on whatever it was that had transpired here. If I'd just paid more attention during the day, I could have thwarted Nasty's detainment.

"Is that portable?" I asked.

"Here," Harry said. He handed the floodlight to me. "Take it as far as you can. I'll get another extension cord."

I held the lamp and walked slowly through the yard, moving the light source to the left and then to the right. From a distance, the floodlight might have looked like a searchlight. With each step, my hopes fell. This was a typical backyard—treated grass but otherwise unremarkable. The patio was a cement slab, with no rust markings left behind to indicate something once there had been removed. The awning over the back patio had seen better days, and once the house's interior was finished, I'd suggest to Lily that we tear it down and outfit the patio with tables and colorful vintage umbrellas. But that wasn't why I was here.

I stepped over the corner of the vegetable garden and froze.

If Gil knew he was moving out of the country and turning the house over to Lily, why would he bother to plant tomatoes?

The sliding door to the house was still open, and I called out Lola's name.

She appeared in the doorway. "Did you find anything?" she asked.

"Maybe. Can you hold this?" I extended the portable floodlight to her.

Lola walked across the yard, her heels puncturing the lawn with each step. She took the floodlight from me.

"Shine it on the shed," I instructed. The floodlight's cord was stretched to its maximum distance. Lola held the light out, and I went to the shed and grabbed one of the shovels propped alongside of it. I rejoined her and handed her the shovel to hold in her spare hand. Then I moved the aluminum tomato cages from where they'd been positioned to the yard behind me. An unexpected breeze tilted the stack, and the cages fell, making more of a ruckus than I'd wanted.

I took the shovel from Lola. "Aim the light at the ground," I said.

"Do you think Gil buried something out here?"

"I don't know. Maybe this is really a vegetable garden. Maybe whoever mows the lawn tends the garden, and Gil forgot to tell them that he was moving."

Lola shivered and wrapped her free arm around herself. She held the floodlight unsteadily.

I placed the tip of the shovel in the dirt, planted my foot on it, then leveraged my body weight to push the shovel deep into the freshly turned dirt. The shovel moved easily through the topsoil. I scooped up a pan of dirt and dumped it to the right of my feet. Then the floodlight went out.

"Hold on there, girlies," Harry said. "You unplugged the thing. Give me a second to reconnect it."

I didn't need the light to keep shoveling dirt out of the gardens, so I plunged the tip of the spade back into the dirt and displaced another couple of panfuls. The ease with which the dirt moved told me it had been placed recently and hadn't had time to settle. After I moved the fourth pan of dirt out, the floodlight came back on, and Lola gasped. The light fell to the ground, and she put both hands to her face.

I picked up the light and flashed it into the hole I'd dug. The light reflected off a purplish-white male face. I'd never met this man, but even with his bloated face and discolored skin, I recognized his bald head and fluffy mustache from the arboretum website.

"I thought you said you found Gil dead at the arboretum," Lola said shakily.

"I did."

"Then what's his body doing here?"

I stared at her, trying to understand her confusion. "That's not Gil," I finally said. "It's his research partner, Ed Bishop."

CHAPTER TWENTY-ONE

"FIND SOMETHING?" HARRY CALLED FROM HIS SIDE OF THE fence.

I turned around and looked at him. I didn't know how to explain what we'd found, but Harry had been instrumental in our discovery, and we had no way to keep this a secret.

After the inevitable call to Detective Sue, Lola and I waited at Harry's house. Turned out he was a night owl, and our visit did little more than keep him from the latest Jack Reacher novel. It was late, and I expected him to offer us coffee, but instead he poured three glasses of bourbon and carried them to the table. Lola swallowed hers in one gulp, and Harry refilled her glass. When I took a sip, I immediately felt a burning sensation in my throat and then my chest. The liquor warmed me, but I didn't think it was the best solution for what was turning out to be a heck of a night.

Lola hadn't asked me how I knew the dead man was Gil's partner, and I hadn't asked why she thought it was Gil. Somewhere in there lay the intertwined threads of the mystery, though, and I couldn't help seeing that both Lola and Ed had borrowed acquaintances' names for speed dating. It was the closest connection back to Nasty that we had, and I wanted Lola to tell her story to Sue and Jerry when they arrived, not to me. I wanted it all to come out in one unedited flow of words.

I set my glass on the table and excused myself to make a couple of phone calls. The people I needed to inform of this latest discovery was stacking up, but Tex came first. He didn't answer. I left him a message that it was going to be a long night and added that he should call me back if he had a chance. I didn't relish the role of bad-news bearer, so I moved on to Connie, arguably the easier call of those on my list.

"Hey, Mad," she answered. "You on your way back?"

"Not exactly. I can't get into things right now, but we're not going to make it back to Tex's place for a few hours. I know that's a massive inconvenience to you, and I'm sorry to have brought you into this."

"Don't sweat it. I found a crib in the spare bedroom. I set it up with cushions from the sofa, and Huxley fell asleep in seconds."

"Tex doesn't have a crib in his spare bedroom."

"It's less of a crib and more of a cage."

"Tex used that to potty train Wojo."

"Oh." She fell silent. "Don't tell Nasty, okay?"

"I think by the time this is all over, Nasty will be thankful you took such good care of her son."

My next call was to Lily.

"Hi," she said. Her voice was edged with sleep. "Is everything okay?"

"I'm sorry to wake you," I said. This time, I shared more details. "We found Ed Bishop's body buried in the tomato gardens behind the house."

"Ed?" Her voice sounded instantly alert. "Gil's partner?"

"Yes. Did you know him well?"

"I've met him a few times, but he wasn't anything more than a passing acquaintance." She thought for a moment. "You know—it's probably nothing."

"What?"

"It's just—hold on." The phone went silent, but the call display indicated we were still connected. I didn't know why she'd asked me to hold on, but I assumed she muted me.

A few seconds later, she came back. "Madison? Are you still there?"

"I'm here."

"David said the boys ran into Ed at the cemetery."

"The day Tex was stung by the bees?"

"Yes. He said he waved, but Ed didn't see him. That has to be a coincidence, right?"

"Does David remember anything else?"

"No, just that Ed was at the cemetery. Hold on again. What?" This time, Lily didn't mute the phone. I turned up the volume so I could overhear her. I heard David's voice, but his words were muffled.

"Madison?" Lily asked. "David said Ed was there when Tex got stung. He asked Ed for his help, and Ed said he had to leave. He said he was late for a meeting, and he got into a van with a couple of men."

"What kind of van?" I asked.

"What kind of a van?" she repeated. By now, I accepted that George was the source of information and Lily was simply the messenger. "A plain white delivery van. You don't think this has something to do with the men who dumped the dirt on your car, do you?"

From my position, it seemed obvious that I did, but knowing that Lily didn't was enough to make me question my attempt to connect dots and tie up loose ends. The night's events had left me keyed up and restless, and this latest information did nothing but intensify the feelings. I didn't answer Lily's question, but no, I didn't think it was a coincidence.

"Your brother is at my place with Effie," I said. "You can head back there if you want, or you can go to Tex's townhouse. Connie's there with Huxley. The only place you shouldn't come is here."

"What about Donna?"

"I think she's still with the police."

"Adam and Gabe are asleep in one of the spare bedrooms. If it's all the same to you, we'll stay here for the night. I don't think she'd mind."

"Okay." I hung up on Lily and was about to head back to the living room when an incoming call from Tex lit up my phone. I answered.

"Hey, Night," he said in a drowsy voice.

"Hi. You sound half-asleep. How do you feel?"

"Like I've been stuffed with cotton. The antihistamines are working, but I can't seem to hold a thought for more than a minute. Where are you?"

"Lola and I are with Lily's new neighbor, Harry." I gave Tex a moment to ask why, and when he didn't, I assumed Sue had called him after I'd called them. "Good guy. He's lived in this development since it was built."

"What's Lo doing there?"

"It's a long, complicated story, and I'm not sure your cotton-stuffed brain can handle it right now. How'd things go with Effie?"

"Good. I pulled the images from your camera and emailed them to Sue. After that, your slave driver had me unpack most of the cartons you had stacked up inside the office. I found something you'll want to see. Left it on your kitchen table."

Headlights flashed through the street-facing windows and stopped in front of Lily's house. I watched Sue and Jerry exit the car and head up the path.

"Okay. Go back to sleep. I'll see you tomorrow."

I found Lola and Harry in the kitchen. Her hands were wrapped around her tumbler, and a thin band of amber coloring inside it indicated she hadn't yet finished this refill. A thick burgundy blanket lay draped over her shoulders, and when I focused on the lines of it, I could tell she was shaking underneath. Her eyes were unfocused. She stared at something across the table from her. Harry had set out a plate of chocolate chip cookies, but they were untouched.

When Harry saw me, he stood. Lola didn't move. Harry gestured for me to join him a few feet away by the dishwasher, and I did.

"Your friend is in a state of shock," he said.

"I don't blame her. She's been seeing the man in the grave, but he lied to her about his identity, so she's dealing with multiple issues."

"Yeah, but this is textbook physical shock. Her breathing is shallow, her pulse is weak, and her skin is clammy. I worked in combat triage for the army. Got too much practice recognizing the symptoms. She needs medical oversight."

I left Harry overseeing Lola and carried the portable floodlight back to Lily's house. As soon as I stepped out through the back door, Sue spotted me. She met me by the back fence like I'd met Harry.

"The last time I saw you was at Ms. Nast's house," she stated. I didn't miss her formal use of Nasty's name. "How'd you end up here?"

"The speed dating clue—it's wrong. Gil wasn't the one who went to speed dating; his partner was." I pointed at the body behind her. "Ed Bishop. He worked on privatized botanical research with Gil at the Lakewood Arboretum. He used his partner's name at speed dating. If you check with the event organizers, they should be able to confirm his identity."

"I'm interested in your actions, not Mr. Bishop's."

"I'm just saying, you detained Nasty earlier tonight, but that conclusion was based on faulty assumptions."

"Madison," she said, interrupting me. "I know you're worried about your friends. That's natural. But I'm conducting an investigation. Don't make this more difficult than it has to be."

I knew Sue was no hack when it came to investigation. She was half of the most respected team of homicide detectives in the state. But I felt like I was on the outside staring into a room with tinted windows and semi-sheer drapes. Nothing was clear.

"Please. Listen. I showed you the clue in Gil's calendar," I said. "When you left, we both thought SD meant San Diego, but I learned that it meant 'speed dating.' I know you figured that out, too—before me. After you detained Donna from the party, I—we—figured it out. Today is Wednesday, so I went to speed dating to see what I could find out."

Sue didn't look pleased.

"Detective Niedermeier, show some heart," I continued. I wanted to repeat what Tex had told me about the men driving the white van filled with dirt, but it wouldn't look good for Tex to admit he'd shared confidential case details with me while under the influence of painkillers, so I stuck to my firsthand knowledge. "You arrived unannounced at a family party and removed the hostess from the premises with no explanation why. You left behind the immediate family member of your boss, along with the two-year-old son of the woman you detained, who happens to be a former police officer. This case is personal on several levels. I wasn't trying to hide anything when I went to the taco restaurant."

Sue pulled her phone out of her pocket and scrolled through a few recent photos until she came to one of me in Connie's MY LIFE MY RULES T-shirt. "Is this you?"

"Yes."

She scrolled to an earlier photo and showed it to me. In it, Connie and I were in various stages of undress in the taco restaurant parking lot. "And this?"

"Yes."

"I could have you arrested for public indecency."

"Oh, come on! I'm wearing a late-fifties bullet bra and panties that come up to my ribcage. There are women at nightclubs in Dallas wearing less than I wear under my clothes."

My response won me Sue's first smile of the night. She put her phone back in her pocket. "I need this one to be clean for the sake of Captain Allen's reputation. Can you respect that?"

I nodded.

I'd wanted Lola's story to come out to Sue in her statement, but my desperation led me to spill it myself. I told her what I knew, holding back any information I'd gained secondhand, like Lily telling me David had seen Ed at the cemetery when Tex was stung. That detail felt relevant, but it also felt a little whisper-down-the-alley, and I'd feel better about that information if it reached Sue from the source. I told her about finding Lola at speed dating, about her pretending to be her sister, about going to Tex's house to try to straighten everything out, and then about coming here. I told her Lola was currently in a state of near-shock at the house next door, and we left Jerry supervising the crime scene techs while I led her and an EMT to Harry's.

Lola was lying on Harry's sofa with the rough burgundy blanket draped over her. Her eyes were open, but she appeared not to be focusing on anything in particular.

"Lola," I said. I gently touched her shoulder and she flinched. I bent down so my face was in her sightline. "Lo, I'm here with Detective Niedermeier. She wants to talk to you about Ed Bishop. You need to tell her what you told me about pretending to be your sister at speed dating. Can you do that?"

Lola pushed herself up so she was sitting. Her wrap dress had come loose, and the edges of her black lace bra were visible at her neckline. I reached forward and adjusted the blanket around her shoulders, and she pulled it tighter around her body as if creating a cocoon to hide from any more bad news.

"Ms. Nast, I'd like one of the EMTs to take a look at you before we talk. Can you follow him to the medical van?"

"Sure," Lola said. She stood and followed the EMT. I started to walk with her, and Sue turned to face me.

"Is there anything you forgot to mention?" Sue asked.

"No."

"Okay. Then I'm going to ask you to leave." She added, in no uncertain terms, that the house was off-limits for decorating, investigating, and relisting with a real estate agent until I heard from her. The team of crime scene techs who arrived shortly after her set up their own floodlights around the perimeter of the yard, lighting the grounds up like a Christmas tree, and I had a feeling the resale value had changed significantly overnight. Not knowing the neighborhood, I couldn't say if it went up or down.

CHAPTER TWENTY-TWO

WHAT TROUBLED ME THE MOST ABOUT THE WHOLE NIGHT WAS Sue's behavior. Normally, she was forthcoming. Understanding. She acknowledged my close relationship with her boss, and she worked with me when she could. When our conversations approached a line that might jeopardize her ongoing investigation, she'd tell me, and I respected that boundary. Sating my curiosity could wait.

But in this case, she treated me differently. The shift was subtle, but it was there. My questions went unanswered. My theories went unchecked. Even my attempts at small talk about how her young partner fared while her regular partner was on vacation were met with only the most minimal of responses. Sue was evading me on purpose, and I didn't think that boded particularly well for Nasty.

I ensured that Lola would be given a ride back to Tex's townhouse, where her car was, and I left.

I was exhausted. This was the biggest problem with my occasional brush with the underbelly of Dallas. Bad guys didn't do bad things in the early morning hours when I was up to swim laps with the seniors at the local pool. I didn't keep nightlife hours. I felt physical fatigue in my joints and muscles and mental fatigue in my mind. I would have curled up on the beanbag chair and driven home in the morning, but Sue made it clear she didn't want me sticking around. My only option was a ride home in a police cruiser. It wouldn't be my first one.

It was close to three when I got home. Tex was asleep on the sofa with Rocky curled up by his knees. Rocky raised his fluffy white head and cocked it to the side. I held my finger up to my lips as if Rocky could understand and ran my other hand over his fur. He set his head back down on his paw and closed his eyes. The movement was enough to wake Tex.

"Hey," he said. He propped himself up on his left arm and rubbed his eyes with his right hand. "What time is it?"

"Three." Moonlight poured through the windows, the only illumination in the room. The swelling from the bee stings was gone from Tex's face, as was the discoloration from his black eye. For the first time since Lily and her boys had arrived in town, Tex looked like Tex. I held my hand out and threaded my fingers through his. "Why are you on the sofa and not the bed?"

"Conked out after my last round of meds. Too tired to climb the stairs."

"Where's Effie?"

"I sent her home at midnight." He reached out for me, but I was too exhausted to do much more than lean against him.

"If it's all the same to you, my body prefers a mattress."

"Is that an invitation?"

"Definitely not."

Tex gave his lazy, sexy smile. Despite his attempts at playfulness, I could tell that he was closer to asleep than awake. He punched his pillow a few times to fluff it back up and then settled back into the cushions. I adjusted the blanket over his body, kissed his forehead, then went upstairs for my own chance at slumber.

* * *

THE NEXT MORNING, I dressed in a yellow and white dress from the estate of Virginia Healy. Virginia had been one of three tellers for the Oakwood State Bank in 1957, and her cheerful wardrobe reflected a desire to brighten customers' lives when they came into her branch. Like all of her ensembles, this one had a matching jacket and hat, both of which were safely preserved in my closet. You just never know when you'll need a head-to-toe yellow polka dot ensemble. I pulled on a pair of yellow Keds and Rocky followed me downstairs.

I found Tex scrambling eggs in my kitchen.

"Must have been a heck of a party," he said. "Did you wake me when you got in?"

"You don't remember?"

He shook his head.

"Then that's the last time I surprise you in one of those outfits from Frederick's of Hollywood," I said.

"Nice try, Night."

I reached across him and pinched a piece of bacon from where it was draining on a pile of paper towels. "The party broke up when your detectives arrived. Didn't Sue tell you?"

Tex froze. He held a rubber spatula in one hand, and a

blob of egg fell off and landed on my yellow tiled floor. "Why'd my detectives show up at Nasty's? Is my sister okay?"

I grabbed a fresh paper towel and mopped up the egg from the floor. "Lily's okay, but Nasty isn't." I grabbed onto a cabinet handle and pulled myself up. I tossed the garbage and turned back to Tex. "I don't know what they told you about the speed dating clue. Hopefully, after they talk to Nasty's sister, they'll get it all straightened out."

Tex looked at me funny. "Nasty's sister? Which one?"

"Lola. Do you know her?"

"Sure. She's like Nasty without the drive." He scooped eggs onto each of the plates, added bacon, then turned off the burner and carried the plates to the table. "What's this about speed dating?"

I glanced from his face to the eggs and back to his face. There was a disconnect between what Tex knew and what I thought Tex knew, and I felt a shaky sensation, deep in my bones. I put my hands on his shoulders to force him to look me in the eye. "Did you or did you not talk to your detectives last night?"

"Sue and Ling?"

"Sue and Jerry. Ling's on vacation, remember?" I studied his face, searching for some sign of understanding. Tex placed his hands on my forearms. We stood like that, staring at each other, for several seconds, until it dawned on me that Tex, who'd spent most of last night either unpacking boxes in my satellite office or zonked out on my sofa, would need more than the highlights reel.

"Sit down."

Tex didn't move.

"Fine." I dropped my arms and sat down, confident that

he'd join me shortly. "Nasty is currently being detained at your police station for the murder of Gil Banks. I found his partner, Ed, buried in the yard behind the house Gil left Lily. David remembers seeing Ed at the cemetery the morning you were stung en masse. Two patrol officers are out looking for the men—repeat offenders, according to you—who dumped the dirt on my car, and Connie is currently babysitting Huxley in the comfort of your townhouse." I took another bite of the strip of bacon I'd carried with me. I savored both the salty taste and the shocked silence before, I suspected, Volcano Tex would erupt.

But Tex had lived through his own cloud of confusion over the past few days. He turned to the living room and glanced at the sheets on the sofa. "How long have I been out?"

"Sit," I said. I pointed at the chair opposite mine. "Eat. If you ask nicely, I'll tell you everything I know."

Tex sat. He glanced at his plate and then pushed it away and crossed his arms. He uncrossed his arms and picked up his fork, ate a scoop of eggs, and set his fork back down. After swallowing, he said, "talk."

It took a little bit of back and forth to find the point where Tex had lost track of the case, which was right around the speed dating clue. "Ed Bishop has been going to speed dating every Wednesday. He's been seeing someone he thought was Nasty, but it was Nasty's sister Lola."

"Let me guess. My detectives followed the same clue but didn't factor in Nasty's sister."

"Right. If I hadn't seen her in the flesh last night, I would have walked away thinking the same thing."

Tex gripped the edge of the table. "Where's Lola now?"

"Lily's new neighbor said she was exhibiting classic signs of shock. When I left her last night, an EMT was checking her over. Sue wanted to talk to her about Gil and Ed, but I didn't get to stick around for that part."

"Wait here." Tex got up, unplugged his phone from the counter, and then made a call. "It's Captain Allen," he barked. "I need a full update on the Gil Banks case." He listened for a few seconds and then spoke again. "I've just corroborated her statement. She's free to go. Tell her a ride is on the way." He hung up and went searching for his sneakers.

I followed him into the living room. "Where are you going?"

"The precinct."

"You're on who knows what medication. I can't let you get behind the wheel."

"I'm not. You're coming with me."

"Me? Why?"

He straightened up. "I need a ride to the precinct. Nasty needs a ride from the precinct to wherever she wants to go. Two birds, one stone."

Tex stormed through the kitchen to the side door. When he was on a mission, few things could stop his forward trajectory. Today, what stopped it was the lack of vehicle.

"Where's your car?" he asked.

"Your place."

"Where's my Jeep?"

"Your place." I grabbed the keys to Lily's moving truck. "It's this or nothing."

"Let's go."

CHAPTER TWENTY-THREE

I DROVE TEX TO THE POLICE STATION AND FOLLOWED HIM inside. Nasty stood by the receptionist's desk. As soon as she saw Tex, her face twisted into a scowl. I would have felt much more popular if I hadn't arrived with him, but it was too late to stagger our entrances.

Tex held out his hand to Nasty. "The police department apologizes for any inconvenience."

Nasty pushed his hand out of the way. She glanced at me and then left. I raised my eyebrows at Tex, and he tipped his head toward the door. "Go."

I didn't wait around for him to change his mind.

I caught up with Nasty in the parking lot. "Get in the moving van. Huxley's at Tex's place."

If I didn't know Nasty, I might not have picked up on the subtle shift in her attitude. It was anxiety, laced with tension, with a side of sleeplessness. This was a woman who was always in control, but thanks to her sister's actions, she'd spent the night in a local detention center. I couldn't help but see the connection between her and Tex. They were each out on a limb, trying to protect their families. The penalties for doing so had been unexpected.

I parked the truck next to Connie's Miata, and Nasty stared out the front window, though she didn't seem focused on anything. She put her hand on my arm. "I knew Lola used my name at speed dating," she said. "We had a big fight about it. When the cops showed up at my house, I knew exactly why they were there."

"You thought—" I twisted to face her. "You knew they were there because of something Lola did, and you didn't correct them. You took the bullet meant for her."

"When I got pregnant, I underestimated how much I could do on my own. Lo took a six-month leave and moved in with me. For the first three months, she gave me time to get to know Huxley, and she handled everything else. After that, she watched him while I got back to work. I couldn't have done any of this without her."

"And now she needs you."

We got out of the truck and entered Tex's house. Sounds of a happy baby came from the living room, and I sincerely hoped we weren't about to discover Huxley sitting in the middle of Wojo's cage.

We didn't. Instead, we found Connie and Lola sitting on the floor with Huxley between them. He took one look at Nasty and cried out with joy. She scooped him up and held him close.

Lola stood up. "Come on, sis. I'll give you a ride back to your place."

Nasty held Huxley, cradling the back of his head with one hand. She seemed to notice Huxley's diaper bag for the first time. She picked up the strap, hung it over her shoulder, and addressed Connie. "Thank you."

"Anytime," Connie answered. She smoothed Huxley's hair away from his face. "He's a dream."

Huxley scrunched up his face, and seconds later the room filled with a not-so-pleasant scent. He let out a loud wail.

Nasty set him on the counter. "Hold up, Lo. We're not leaving yet."

* * *

THERE'S something about a baby that kept the four of us from focusing on something as trivial as a murder investigation. After Lola and Nasty left, Connie drove me back to my place. She dropped me out front and waited until I was safely inside before driving away.

I felt a hollow emptiness deep in my core. I hadn't seen Tex around Lily until recently, but for the first time since knowing him, I saw desperation. I saw him wanting to protect her, the same way he'd once tried to protect me before we reached an impasse and then an understanding that we couldn't save each other. But there was a difference between love and family. I knew it, because I'd lost my family and had had to learn to go on without them, to provide everything for myself that I might have expected them to provide for me. I'd become an island, and, ironically, it had been Tex who rowed up in a rescue boat to save me from a lifetime of self-isolation.

It was late, or early, depending on which side of eight a.m. you normally saw, and I should have gone to bed. But my nervous system was alert with anxiety and adrenaline, so I sat at the kitchen table and sorted through the buildup of mail.

A small white envelope sat by my place mat. My name had been scripted onto the front of it, as had some abstract doodles. Something about the handwriting tickled a memory deep in the recesses of my mind. I picked up the envelope. Underneath was a note in Tex's handwriting: *Found this while working next door. Thought you'd want to see it.*

I switched on the kitchen light and then slid a letter opener under the sealed corner and sliced through the brittle paper. The card inside was stiff. It showed an illustration of big, loopy, colorful daisies and the word "Congratulations." I opened the card and, before reading the note scrawled inside, saw the signatures. *Love always, Mom and Dad.*

My parents must have bought this card before the car accident that killed them. It happened while I was in college. I'd taken a semester off and never returned to complete my degree.

I resisted the urge to set the card down and pretend I hadn't seen it. I'd spent the past thirty-some years building a life on the shaky ground I'd been left standing on after the car accident. So much of me—who I was today—had been trapped in amber back then, perpetuated to this day by a wardrobe and business model that fit an outdated narrative.

I opened the card back up and read handwriting I hadn't seen in decades.

Congratulations, Madison! We're so proud of you. We may not always be with you, but you'll never be alone. Love always, Mom and Dad.

It had been forever since I'd been that twenty-year-old woman whose life was shattered by the sudden loss of her family unit. I'd blocked the memories of those days in the aftermath. I hadn't arranged a memorial, or submitted an obituary to the newspaper, or purchased a cemetery plot. The cremation and distribution of my parents' ashes had been thoroughly rote because allowing myself to process what had happened had felt like more weight than I could bear at the time. I'd built my entire company around reusing the items originally owned by people who bought mid-century furnishings when they were readily available, and I'd convinced myself this was my way of honoring the original owners' lives, yet I'd never once gone through the estate I'd inherited. I kept it all in a storage unit sight unseen. To be dealt with at a later date when I was ready.

I'd never be ready.

I set the card on the table and pushed it out of reach while a tidal wave of tears spilled down my face. I was a polar cap melting, touched by the two people who I'd never expected to hear from again. And instead of being pulled down into a pit of darkness, I felt as if something inside me had cracked open.

I carried the card with me to the sofa, where Tex's makeshift bedding had been pushed aside. I sat, still feeling faint warmth on the sheets from his body. Rays of sun spilled into the windows, and I felt warm. Comforted. Safe. For years, I'd been so scared of being left behind that I'd convinced myself I could keep the world at arms' length; I'd wanted so badly to belong to something that I'd created my own world and, little by little, allowed people in. It had taken so much of my energy to protect myself from ever letting that kind of loss define me again, but I was nowhere near being alone.

DIANE VALLERE

I kicked off my yellow sneakers and pulled the covers up over my dress. I closed my eyes and felt the memory of belonging to something. For the first time in decades, I felt the warmth and love I'd had in that family unit back when I had a family.

Ever since Lily arrived in Dallas, I'd tried to understand Tex's actions. I'd volunteered to help out and gone along with the flow, but I hadn't truly understood what Tex feared losing because I hadn't let myself mourn my own loss. And I'd maintained a "so-what?" attitude. Lily was as much of an adult as the rest of us were; she could take care of herself just like I had. But no one had mandated that I do it all on my own. No one had said life had to be an uphill battle after that car accident—no one but me.

Eventually, I got up and went next door. I sat at my desk and stared at the satellite office's interior. What had started out as a possible new showroom next door to my house had become a glorified storage unit, housing my expanded inventory. Effie, who was always looking for more responsibility, had gotten her arms around this, too, learning how to identify makers' marks and cross-referencing items in her inventory database. She'd been so effective at her job that I had a hard time thinking of new projects for her. These last few days working for Nasty had come at an opportune time.

I leaned back in my chair and propped my feet on my desk. The heel of my sneaker tore the page off my scratchpad, and I sat back up to make sure I hadn't destroyed an invoice.

It wasn't an invoice. It was a pro/con list written in Effie's handwriting. She hadn't provided details of her decision, but as I scanned the list of pros, it was obvious. Nasty had a job opening at Big Bro Security, and she'd offered it to Effie. Things like *higher salary, advancement opportunities, work in tech* filled the left side of the list. At least seven bullets were listed.

There was only one entry on the con side: *Madison is like family.*

As soon as I read that, something inside me broke. My heart cracked open, and a thousand beams of light shot out. I wasn't alone—I'd never been alone. I was surrounded by friends, partners, colleagues, and lovers. Tex, Connie, Effie, Jimmy, even Nasty—they were my family. Not the one I might have had if things had been different thirty years ago but the one I'd created by building a life on my own. I had never been on my own; I just hadn't noticed that at the time. All the people I interacted with were like guardrails, keeping me from veering too far off on my own, forcing me to interact with them, throwing me lifelines. Even the doors that had closed for me had kept me on this path, bringing me to this moment. It was all working out, all the time, whether I paid attention or not. Whether I forced the issue or not. Whether I wanted it to or not.

Now, more than ever, I wanted to do something for the people who'd become my family. Two days ago, I'd told Lily I'd handle her meeting with the high school principal on her behalf, In light of everything that had transpired, I'd forgotten all about that promise until now. Keeping it was the least I could do.

CHAPTER TWENTY-FOUR

THE LAKEWOOD PREPARATORY SCHOOL WAS A COUPLE OF miles east of Thelma Johnson's house, and I parked in a visitor's space. It was shortly after one. The school offered a student curriculum from K-12, making the place a veritable one-stop shop for parents like Lily who were already juggling more than one person should have to handle. I got out of my car, aware that a layer of dirt still clung to its exterior, unlike the shiny luxury cars that filled the other spaces in the lot, including a red Lexus that was parked in a space close to the door marked Reserved.

The door to the school opened, and Franklin Rich looked out. He glanced to the left and right, and then greeted me. His dress shirt was unbuttoned by the collar, and his sleeves were cuffed. "Coming this way?" he asked. He smiled politely.

"I think so," I said. I scaled the stairs and entered the building. The hallways were empty, and the classroom doors were shut. Posters painted in craft paint had been tacked along a strip of cork just below eye level.

I got the sense that Franklin didn't remember meeting me, so I reintroduced myself. "I'm here to see you," I said. "We met at a cookout for Lily Allen and her boys."

Relief showed on his face. "I knew you looked familiar, but I couldn't remember who you were or where we met. I meet so many parents I sometimes have a hard time keeping track."

I extended my hand, and he held his up in a hands-off manner. "You don't want to shake hands with the principal of a K-12 prep school unless you see him use hand sanitizer." He reached around to the wall and squirted a blob of clear gel into his hands. "Life lesson," he added. After he rubbed the gel into his hand, he extended his own hand, which I shook.

"Lily's been—she wanted—" I grasped at words to explain her absence. I didn't know if the discovery of Ed Bishop's body had made the local news or if the detectives had managed to keep it quiet for a news cycle, but introducing gossip at the local prep school didn't seem like the way to ensure her kids got a clean start. "She has a lot on her plate."

"I can only imagine. Here, come with me to my office." Franklin led the way down the hall to the principal's office. I followed him through a frosted-glass door and sat on the opposite side of his desk. "Is this about the boys' transcripts?"

"Yes."

Franklin leaned forward, dug a few layers down in the wire inbox that sat on the corner of his desk, then pulled out a thick folder. He opened it and scanned the contents and then handed it to me. "I admit, at first I thought we were about to admit a prodigy to our school."

"I don't understand." I opened the folder and was surprised to find a sheath of botanical research notes. Slowly, I flipped through the pages. This was what Gil had left behind for Lily at the arboretum the day we'd found his body. These were the pages that had been printed and deleted from Gil's—or Ed's—computer. Did it matter at this point? I closed the folder and set it on my lap, sure of only one thing: I needed to get this information to Tex.

"That's what you came for, isn't it?" Franklin pointed at the folder.

"Yes. Of course. Lily mixed up the transcripts with some documents from her ex-husband's research lab. I'll be needing to get these back." I paused. "What about the transcripts?"

"David brought them in earlier today. It's a shame about the baseball team, though."

"Don't tell me the boys can't play because their transcripts were late," I asked, feeling guilty for having taken so long to complete Lily's favor.

"The younger ones are fine, but we still haven't found a coach for the high school team." He tapped his fingers on his blotter a few times and then shrugged. "I told David to hang in there and keep practicing. These things have a way of sorting themselves out. You wouldn't be interested, would you?"

"Me? I own a decorating studio. I'm not qualified to coach a high school baseball team."

"I don't know about that. I've seen you pitch."

I smoothed out the skirt of my dress and said, "Yes. Well,"

as if that would effectively end our conversation. "I'm sure you'll find someone more suited to the task."

Franklin leaned back in his chair and it creaked. "How is Lily holding up?"

"It's been a lot to take. I'm sure she expected to have her plans finalized by now. Moving is always more work than it seems like it's going to be."

"She's a trooper, that one," he said. "Tell her the boys will be in good hands here."

"I will," I said. I clutched the folder of research notes to my chest tightly and thanked the principal again, eager to leave. I let myself out of his office and hurried back out to my car when I heard Franklin calling my name.

"Madison!"

I looked up.

Franklin jogged down the stairs with a backpack in his hand. "I almost forgot. David left this behind when he came to see me. I was going to drop it by the house, but I didn't know if they'd moved in yet. Can I trust you to see that he gets it?"

"Of course." I placed the folder and my handbag in my car and met Franklin halfway. I took the backpack from him and something sticky transferred onto my hand. I pulled my hand away and looked at my palm. Something shiny had transferred onto my skin.

"I feel strongly about protecting our students' privacy, so I didn't look inside, but it seems as if something might have spilled." He held out a folded newspaper. "You might want to set it on this to keep your seats clean." He looked past me at my Alfa Romeo, dirt coating and all.

With as much grace as I could muster, I took the

209

newspaper. "Very considerate. Thank you." I shook out the newspaper and lined the passenger seat with it. Then I set the backpack on top of the seat, climbed into my car, and drove away.

Ever since Lily and the boys arrived in Dallas, my life had been topsy-turvy, and from the looks of it, things weren't about to calm down anytime soon. I'd planned to work on Lily's house this week, but even that was off the table, thanks to the body in the backyard. I couldn't help feeling like we were all victims of a crime we still didn't understand.

I was back home in a matter of minutes. I let Rocky out into the yard and called Tex. "It's me," I said. "How's your sister?"

"She's fine. She's calmer than I am. She keeps saying not to worry—it's finally over. I swear she's on antidepressants."

"I can't imagine what it's like to fight with someone for ten years and then have it all just stop. No closure, no resolution. Just done. Gil must have really done a number on her," I said. "Everything that's happened, and the only thing she sees is that she's finally free of Gil."

"I keep waiting for the other shoe to drop. Lack of resolution tends to come back and haunt people. It's always better to have closure."

"Right." I thought about the card from my parents and how finding it thirty years ago might have given me some much-needed closure. And then I thought about how every decision I'd made since then had brought me to this point, and I knew, no matter how much I missed my family, no matter how dark some of those days had been, if I had the chance to do it all over again, I wouldn't change a thing.

While Rocky ran around the yard, a bumblebee zigged

close to me. I ducked and swatted it away. I'd never been as aware of bees as I was now, since I'd seen the damage they could do to Tex. The bee flew away and hovered around my car.

"If it's all the same to you, I'm going to spend the night working at my studio. I've left the windows blacked out for two days now. People are going to start to think I went out of business."

"Sure."

"And tell Lily I have David's backpack. He left it at the school earlier today."

"Thanks, Night."

I disconnected and sat on the swing while allowing an infrequent breeze to blow against my face. I wanted to relax and give in to the promise of April, the hint of spring before the Dallas humidity claimed the weather reports. I wanted to collect the boys and take them to a field to play catch, to get lost in a day of hooky. But I couldn't help it—something wasn't right. Lily may have thought her troubles were over, but they weren't. Not by a long shot. And the more I thought about it, the more it felt like I had a pebble in my shoe. I couldn't relax. I couldn't shake the anxiety.

I'd been involved in homicide cases where it appeared that multiple people had motives. It was Tex's job to separate the red herrings from the real evidence and figure out which of those suspects was the one that committed the crime. Gil's murder didn't feel like that. This felt more about the Why. Why kill a botanist? Why was Gil trying to leave the country? Why leave his estranged wife and four sons a house with a backyard crime scene? Why now?

Gil had been trying to disappear. Was it that difficult to

believe his killer would too? If Gil's presence was a threat to someone, then was the threat now gone? It all seemed so convoluted. If Gil hadn't been married to Tex's sister, if I hadn't promised to help her while he was recovering from the havoc wreaked by her boys, if I had a bigger job on my calendar, I would've had no reason to get involved. The write-up about Gil would have been little more than a second or third page article in the paper. But Tex's words echoed as a refrain in my mind: family was different. And this was his family, and until we knew why someone had murdered Gil, I couldn't shake the notion that Lily and her boys were in danger too.

I went inside my house, got Rocky's leash, then came out and clipped it on and loaded him into my car. He licked the strap of David's backpack.

"No, Rocky!" I picked up the pack and moved it to the back seat. A clear, tacky substance transferred onto my fingers. I turned my hand over, flicked two tiny ants off it, then picked up the backpack and examined it more closely. This time, I saw a pool of small black ants on the floor by the backpack and a few crawling on the strap.

I dropped the pack and stepped back. My hand was sticky again. I raised it to my nose and sniffed. It was a combination of floral nuances and natural sweetness that I instantly recognized. The reality of what I'd just discovered took form. What was the saying I was looking for? You could catch more flies with honey than vinegar. But it wasn't flies that troubled me. It was bees.

With less respect for David's privacy than the principal at Lakewood Prep had, I unzipped the backpack, peered inside, and found a half-empty jar of honey.

CHAPTER TWENTY-FIVE

From the first day the boys arrived in Dallas, they'd sidelined Tex with an accidental black eye and a practical joke that led to embarrassing bathroom issues. But this—this indicated something worse. Would David, the quiet and responsible seventeen-year-old, really use a jar of honey to lure bees to sting his uncle? Did he hold some sort of resentment against Tex—the new dominant male in their lives? Did he know about Tex's allergy?

I drove to my showroom and parked out back. It was after hours, but Jimmy's pickup truck was in my regular space. I carried David's backpack into my office and unclipped Rocky's leash. He took off for the front of the studio and returned a few seconds later with Jimmy in tow.

"Hey, boss," Jimmy said. "I guess you heard about the project house, huh?"

"Heard what?" I asked, more curious about how he had heard the news than a rehash of the news itself.

"The hardwood floors are rotted all the way through." He

leaned against the hallway wall. "Tough break for the cop's sister."

Sometimes my world got so small it seemed as if everybody I spoke to had a thin connection to a case. This was not one of those times. "Jimmy, when did you leave the house yesterday?"

"I worked until eleven. Why?"

"You did not work until eleven. I know this because I was there at nine fifty-five, and if you were there when I was there, we wouldn't be talking about the rotted floors."

"Did I leave the lights on?"

"Jimmy."

"Oh, all right. I knocked off at six thirty. But I was still on the clock! I mean, I left, but I was still working."

Now I was just curious. "On what?"

"On a new idea for the living room." Jimmy chewed his lip. "I was going to talk to you about it today, but—never mind."

"What is it?"

Jimmy sighed, and with his exhale came a drop of his tense shoulders. "I'm reading a book on Dorothy Draper. She did these signature black-and-white floors. Since the hardwood is shot, you'll need some other kind of floor, and I thought you could put down a concrete slab and then mimic a black-and-white floor with carpet squares. It'll be durable, and if the boys—well, if anything happens to it, Lily can replace a square instead of having to replace the whole thing."

I stared at Jimmy. He shifted his weight and pushed his hair out of his face.

"Dorothy Draper?" I asked.

"She's a famous decorator. I thought you'd know her. She did the Greenbriar Hotel in West Virginia after World War II—"

I suppressed a smile. "I know who she is," I said.

"Yeah, well, I've been reading up on decorators ever since I got this job. And Effie showed me your portfolio of completed jobs, and I've never seen you do anything with black and white floors. And I know you usually model your interiors after Doris Day movies, but the Greenbriar officially reopened in 1948, and that's the same year as Doris Day's first movie, which means it's the right era, right?"

"Yes, that is correct."

"It was just an idea," he said.

"It's a good idea." I barely hesitated before plowing ahead with an idea of my own. "Jimmy, how would you like to take point on the living room of the house? I've got the rest of the interior to design, and it would be a big help."

"For real?" he asked, looking up at me from under his overgrown bangs. He seemed so surprised by my suggestion that he didn't even try to shake his hair out of his face.

"For real."

Jimmy grinned. "Thanks, boss."

"There's just one thing."

"What?"

"There was a body found buried in the yard behind the house. The police have restricted access to the property until they release the crime scene. The victim was the research partner of the man who gave the house to Lily, so it might be some time until we're able to resume the renovation."

The color drained from Jimmy's face. "When did all that happen?" he asked with a gulp.

"Around the same time you said you were there working last night."

Jimmy was just as happy not to learn the details about the discovery of Ed Bishop's body as I was not to relay them, so we dropped the subject. In truth, I was happy to have Jimmy in the showroom, not because I intended to load him down with more work but because I didn't want to be alone. I couldn't shake the notion that somewhere along the way, we'd all been duped.

After a crash course in my inventory system, I left Jimmy in the office with access to my design programs and database. In a short time, he'd become more than an experimental hire. He fit into Mad for Mod in a way Effie never had, not for lack of wanting but because he had a natural interest in decorating. It benefited me that he'd gotten suspended, since for the next few days, I had him at my disposal. I liked this new side of him and wanted to encourage it.

Twice now I'd attempted to decorate my showroom windows, and both times the display sold before I had a chance to finish it. This wouldn't be the first time I had to get creative and decorate my windows on the fly, and it wouldn't be the last.

I looked around the interior to get an idea, and I spotted a discarded pile of catcher's mitts. I'd forgotten all about digging them out for the boys. I sat in a chair next to the box and dug through it, pulling out worn leather mitts, discolored softballs, and well-loved bats. A long time ago, I'd played softball in high school, just like Lily's boys did now. Like many memories I'd pushed away, those came back, as fresh as if they'd happened yesterday. And with them came my inspiration.

I carried the box of baseball equipment to the window and climbed behind the black curtain that kept my work from curious eyes but I was more in need of attention than privacy. I removed the curtain, and traces of today's sunlight filled the space.

First thing first: I needed a wall treatment. A coat of paint would do the trick, but I'd have to leave it overnight to dry before I could finish, and I was too motivated for that. I left the windows and pulled several large sheets of gatorboard out of my craft closet, along with a hole punch and a ball of red yarn. I punched holes into the edge of the gatorboard and then threaded the holes with the yarn to mimic the lacing on a baseball. I carried the makeshift room divider to the window and checked it for fit. The board required a little trimming with an X-ACTO knife, a skill I'd picked up a long time ago, but soon, I had a perfect fit.

Once the backdrop was in place, I brought in the baseball bats and positioned them vertically like large wooden plant stems. I secured them to the backdrop with invisible wires and topped each one off with a worn baseball mitt clutching an equally worn ball. By the time I finished, it looked as if I'd grown a baseball-themed garden.

One of the benefits of buying out hundreds of estates over the years was the accumulation of items that might otherwise never be used. I already knew I had a bounty of picnic baskets at my disposal, thanks to Effie's inventory database. I also knew I had more than one broken wooden table. I left the window and found Jimmy out back with Rocky.

"How's it going?" Jimmy asked.

"Great." I glanced around the parking lot. "What happened to that busted wooden table?"

"I took it to the Cinderella house," he said. "I thought I could use the wood to make a new mantel."

"I suppose that means you took your table saw there, too, doesn't it?"

He nodded.

"Okay, give me a moment." I went back inside and called the police precinct. I could have called Tex and let him handle things the way he saw fit, but this felt like a time to follow official channels. The regular desk manager, a mystery writer who showed up with the motivation to add a realistic description of the police department to her work-in-progress, was at a mystery convention in Maryland. I didn't recognize the voice of the person subbing for her, so I simply asked to speak to Detective Niedermeier. My call was transferred.

"Detective Tsu," answered a voice I hadn't heard in a while.

"Ling?"

"Madison?"

"I thought you were on vacation?"

"I am. I was. Got shelves up in my den and repainted all my doors. But then I heard you found yourself a body in Captain Allen's sister's yard, and now it's all hands on deck."

"I thought Sue said you went to the Rock and Roll Hall of Fame?"

"That's what I told her. She never would have left me alone if she knew I was in town. Why'd you call the front desk?"

"I have a predicament. My part-time contractor has been working on Captain Allen's sister's house, and he left his table saw in the living room—"

"Say no more. Sue said her team finished processing the crime scene about an hour ago. You want me to meet you out there?"

"Sure," I said. Then I hung up and spoke to Jimmy.

"I'd love for you to cut the broken table in half so I can use it in the windows," I told him, "but we'll save time if you get the table and I get the saw."

"You're going back to the house where you found the body?"

"That is where you left it, right?"

"Right. I just—man. I wish I were as tough as you. Amber's never going to fall for a guy like me."

CHAPTER TWENTY-SIX

I HAD TO ADMIT, THE LAST THING ON MY MIND WAS JIMMY'S relationship troubles. Sue had effectively shut me out of the investigation, but Ling might not know that. And Ling was the one who'd meet me at the house where Ed had been buried out back. And as I drove, I tried to line up my thoughts, to figure out what I needed to know and how best to ask the questions without seeming too eager.

My prep work was in vain. Ling, Sue, and Jerry stood together on the front yard. Ling waved and Sue shook her head. Jerry had his arms crossed over his chest. I parked and approached them.

"You might as well tell her," Sue said to Jerry. "She's going to read about it in tomorrow's paper." She turned to me. "Young Jerry here solved his first case."

Jerry turned back to me. "Gil Banks and Ed Bishop were growing ephedra at the arboretum."

"Ephedra? For diet pills?" I asked.

"For methamphetamines," Jerry said.

Sue added, "Ms. Nast gave us the address for an apartment not far from here that was leased to Ed Bishop. There was enough equipment there to confirm production."

"This has to do with drugs?" I asked. I looked from Jerry to Sue to Ling.

Ling held up her hands. "Don't look at me. I was checking out guitars in Cleveland."

"Oh please," Sue said. "You were installing a new deck." At Ling's surprised expression, Sue rolled her eyes. "What kind of detective do you think I am?"

"So that's it?" I asked. "Case closed?"

"The homicide case is closed, and the rest of it went to the narcotics bureau. They're working concurrent with the DEA and the FBI." Sue glanced at Jerry, who looked none too happy about this last fact. "Once Wonderkid here finishes writing up his case notes, our part is over."

"It sounds like congratulations are in order," I told Jerry. "If you crack all of your cases like you cracked this one, you're going to become a meme too."

Jerry blushed. "It was nothing."

Sue playfully jabbed his upper arm. "Good going, partner," she said. "And here I thought I was going to have to carry you."

I wasn't going to lie. In the past, I'd been somewhat involved in the catching of criminals. Satisfaction came with hearing someone confess to their crimes and then using that confession to make sure they would go away for a long time. It helped me understand why Tex was compelled to do what he did. That insight may have helped us improve the odds of maintaining a healthy relationship despite the circumstances of our lives.

"So," I said, attempting to bring the Jerry-lovefest back around to the business at hand. "Does one of you need to come inside with me while I get the table saw?"

"Not necessary," Sue said. She held out a set of keys and dropped them into my palm. "We combed the backyard this morning and then went over every inch of this house. The evidence we needed to wrap this thing up came from the arboretum and the apartment. They were either planning to use this place as a front or a distraction. Aside from the body out back, the property came back clean."

"Thanks, I guess," I said.

"Don't thank me yet. You haven't seen what a team of field techs with fingerprint dust can do to a house while working under a time constraint."

"Any of you want to stick around and help me clean?" I asked hopefully,

"Not me," Ling quipped. "I'm still on vacation."

We went our separate ways. I thought it interesting that all three detectives left before I had opened the front door— at least I thought it interesting until I saw the layer of black film that covered every surface of the house. Even the carpet that Jimmy had pulled up and left in a ball in the middle of the living room floor had been unfolded and now showed a footprint pattern that illustrated the amount of back-and-forth traffic there had been inside.

No one would have blamed me if I grabbed Jimmy's table saw and left. It was the reason I was there, after all. But something about the quiet of this demolition-condition property felt peaceful. This whole week, I'd watched people get displaced. Lily and her boys, from the move-in-ready property to Tex's townhouse to Nasty's mansion. Tex, from his townhouse to a hospital bed to my sofa. Effie, from her desk at Mad for Mod to Nasty's IT department. Jimmy, from his school to this house to Effie's desk. Nasty, from her mansion to a temporary cell at the police station. We were individuals who rotated in circles, moving around, trying to find where we belonged.

If, for every action, there was an equal and opposite reaction, then Gil had set all our activities into motion when he made plans to give Lily the house and disappear. He'd claimed he'd received a lucrative job offer outside the country, but that no longer seemed true. He'd been using his job at the arboretum to produce small batches of addictive drugs with the intent to distribute. It was all so difficult to believe. The police might have wrapped up the case, but I still had questions.

Like who killed whom? If Gil killed Ed and buried him behind the house, then who killed Gil? And if Ed killed Gil, then who buried Ed? I understood that there were details I might never know, but something was missing from the bigger picture. A third party. Someone who would have benefitted if *both* Gil and Ed were dead.

A distributor.

I wandered through the house. After everything that had happened, I didn't know if Lily would still want to live here. There was enough structural damage to keep Jimmy working for months, which meant Lily and the boys would need a home in the meantime. Even I, a lifelong proponent of renovation over demolition, of preservation over modernization, could make an argument for blowing the place up and starting from scratch. An air of depression clung to every surface of this house and not just because of the fingerprint dust left behind.

No matter what Lily decided to do, the house wasn't going to clean itself. I went into the kitchen in search of a bucket and rags. I found my forgotten sketchpad on the kitchen counter. I flipped it open and scanned the notes I'd written on an earlier walk-through. *Star Trek* theme for David. Farrah Fawcett poster for George. Baseball theme for Adam and Gabe. That felt like forever ago. Aside from Jimmy's idea for the living room, I had no inspiration whatsoever. I was more interested in going back to my studio and finishing up my windows than trying to reconceive a house that seemed cursed.

I tore those pages from the notepad then ripped them in half. I opened and closed a couple of cabinets until I found a small wastepaper bin. I was about to toss the papers inside when I noticed a grocery store receipt inside the trash bin. I pulled out the piece of paper and smoothed it against the counter. The purchaser had paid cash for three items: a jar of honey, a pair of gloves, and a bundle of rope.

Something about the items on the receipt bothered me. I went outside to my car and brought David's backpack inside. I unzipped the backpack and held it open. Alongside the half-empty jar of honey were a bundle of rope and a pair of gardening gloves. I pulled a stack of notebooks out from underneath the miscellany and flipped each one open. They were brand-new and unmarked.

I lined up the items and tried to make sense of them. David had been with Tex every time something had happened. He had access to car keys and a driver's license, which gave him autonomy. He was the eyewitness to Ed

Bishop at the cemetery, and he'd been at Nasty's when the police showed up.

Was I really thinking this? Did I believe a seventeen-year-old boy had killed his father and his business partner, that that boy had buried one of the men in his new backyard, that he'd kept his police captain uncle preoccupied with a series of health issues, all in the name of—what? Protecting his mother? Protecting his brothers? Punishing his dad for a lifetime of abandonment?

I picked up my phone to call Tex but changed my mind. I called Lily instead.

"It's Madison," I said. "Is your brother with you?"

"Yes. He's playing catch with Adam. Do you need him?"

"No, actually, I wanted to ask you a question about David. Has he been acting differently?"

"David's the last one I worry about. He minds his own business and never gets into trouble. Why?"

I leaned back and stared at the items on the table. From the moment I'd met the boys, David had been the least threatening of the bunch. But was this a case of the quiet one hiding the biggest secret?

"I don't know," I said. "Did Tex tell you I have his backpack?"

"Since when does my brother carry a backpack?"

"Not Tex's. David's."

"David doesn't have a backpack either."

"Yes, he does. He left it behind at the school. Franklin gave it to me when I dropped off the boys' transcripts."

"That's odd," she said. "He must have just gotten it."

"Let him know so he doesn't worry."

"I'll tell him when I see him."

"He's not with you?"

"No, he said he was going to meet up with some new friends."

I thanked Lily and hung up. That piece of friction was there again. Something wasn't right.

While I'd been sitting at the dining room table, the sun had dropped. The back curtains had been pulled closed, and the interior was dark. I went to the sliding door and pushed the curtains aside. Like the inside of the house, the backyard showed signs of the police's presence. The dirt had been dug up, and a gaping hole was now where the tomato garden had been. Something troubled me, but I couldn't figure out what. I slid the door open and stepped outside.

As I stood in the backyard, near the freshly turned dirt, I felt an impending sense of doom. I walked to the potting shed. The rusted padlock I'd seen days ago had been replaced with a new one. For all of the mess the detectives had left inside the house, it seemed unusual that they would have removed the padlock to search the shed and then replace it with a new one.

And then I heard a weak groan coming from inside the shed, and the only question that mattered was how to get the lock off the door.

CHAPTER TWENTY-SEVEN

I GRABBED ONE OF THE SHOVELS AND BROUGHT IT DOWN against the padlock. The pan of the shovel bounced off the lock. I raised the shovel again, to no avail. On the third attempt, the backyard filled with illumination from Harry's floodlight.

"What the devil is going on over there now?" he asked.

"Harry, it's Madison. I need to get into this shed."

"You sure do decorate at odd hours."

I tossed the shovel to the ground, grabbed the padlock, and yanked on it even though the action was futile. "This isn't about decorating. There's someone trapped inside."

"Stay right there." Harry went inside his house and came back with his shotgun. "Stand clear."

"No!" I cried. "That's too dangerous."

Harry tapped on the door with the butt end of his shotgun. "Somebody in there?"

"Yes," said a faint female voice. "David passed out. Help me."

I didn't waste time thinking about what had transpired to get not one but two teenagers into the potting shed. "Stand away from the door," I said.

"I can't move him," she said.

"Hold on." I looked at Harry and nodded. He aimed his shotgun at the padlock and fired at a safe angle. The blast knocked him back a few steps and blew the entire locking mechanism clear off the door.

I pushed the door inside and found a pretty blonde huddled against an unconscious David Banks. I reached my hand out and helped her to her feet. Harry draped David's body over his shoulder and carried him to his house. I kept my arm around the blonde and guided her behind Harry.

Once we were inside Harry's place, I found where Harry kept his glasses. I filled two with water then handed one to the girl.

She swallowed a few sips and then asked, "Can I use your phone?"

My cell was next door at Lily's place. "Harry?"

"Cordless is on the counter."

The girl took the phone and dialed a number from memory. "Mom?" she said. "It's Amber. I'm okay." She glanced up at me, and I held out my hand for the phone. She handed it to me.

"Hello?" I called. "This is Madison Night. I'm with your daughter. She was locked inside a potting shed with—another student." I gave Amber's mother the address and then added, "She needs to go to the hospital to be checked for shock." I handed the phone back to Amber.

"Don't tell Dad. Please?" She paused. "It wasn't David's fault. It wasn't!"

I left Amber on the phone and joined Harry. He held David's wrist and stared at the sweeping second hand on his watch.

"His pulse is getting stronger," Harry said. "Wait with him. I'm going to get a few more blankets."

I joined David on the sofa. His eyes fluttered open, closed, and open again. He looked around the interior of the house and then turned to me. Recognition hit him.

"Where's Amber?" he asked.

"She's on the phone with her mother. Do you want to tell me what happened between the cookout and you being in that shed out back?"

David shifted uncomfortably. "I met Amber the other day when I went to the school. I wanted to hang out with her, but her dad's super protective of her. He won't let her go out with anybody he hasn't met. So I had this idea to get him out of the picture."

I felt my forehead scrunch and, involuntarily, I leaned away from David. He detected my shift in body language. "David, what did you do with Amber's father?"

"Huh?" he asked, and then, seemed to realize I suspected the worst. He looked embarrassed. "I invited him to the cookout. I knew if he was there, he wouldn't be able to keep an eye on her. I saw you talking to him so I called her from inside and snuck out when she got there."

I felt a buzzing sensation. Things were coming into focus, but before I made any big leaps, I had to make sure the kids were okay. "Where's her car?" I asked.

"When we got here, there were cop cars parked in front. She parked around the side of the block and we cut through the yard behind mine to see what was going on. Someone dug up the backyard, and the shed was open."

It hadn't been that long since the detectives handed the keys over to me, but what had Sue said? They started out back and then worked their way through the house. The condition of the interior was enough to tell me they'd been inside for hours. Of course they hadn't relocked the shed with a new padlock. The collection of evidence was their job; the condition of the property was mine.

David didn't go into details about what he and Amber were hoping to find when they came to the house, and I didn't bother asking questions. This was the longest conversation I'd had with him, and both he and Amber had been through a traumatic experience. Neither of them needed a lecture on the perils of necking in a shed full of rusty gardening equipment.

"How did the door get locked?"

"We didn't know we weren't alone," David said. "I pulled the door closed, and then we heard someone moving around outside. Amber was really scared. I told her to be quiet. She backed away from the door as far as she could and hid behind the lawnmower. I was trying to be brave, so I opened the door to see who was there. Somebody shoved me back inside and locked us in."

"Did you get a clear look at whoever did it?"

"No," David said. "It all happened too fast."

"It's okay," I said. "You're both okay now."

It frightened me more than I wanted to admit that by keeping David in the dark about what was going on, he'd put himself and Amber in danger—more than any of us could have known if my new suspicions were correct.

Harry came over to check on us. He held out a phone. "You should call your mother," he told David.

"He should call the police," I replied.

"Moms come first," Harry said.

David looked at me.

"Call your mother," I instructed. "I'll get my bag and take you wherever home is tonight."

I didn't need to overhear David telling Lily where he was or why. There would be ample time to get that story from Lily—or, more likely, from Tex. But there was one piece of information I did need to tell Tex, and it couldn't wait. Not if we wanted closure.

I left Harry's and reentered Lily's house through the sliding back door. I thought I'd left my phone on the kitchen counter, but it wasn't there. I went to the landline mounted on the wall and called Tex.

"Yo, Night," he said.

"Are you with Lily?"

"She's inside. I'm cleaning the grill."

"Listen to me. I'm at the house on Cinderella Lane," I said in a rush. "David's been locked in the potting shed with his girlfriend, Amber." I turned around and stared at Jimmy's table saw, which rested next to my lineup of rope and honey on the end of the table. There was an empty space between the two, and it took me too long to remember the gloves and what their absence meant. "It's the school principal. Franklin Rich. I'm willing to bet he's behind the murders of Gil Banks and Ed Bishop. Send Jerry and Sue to arrest him."

"That's not going to work for me," said Franklin Rich, stepping out from the shadows.

CHAPTER TWENTY-EIGHT

PRINCIPAL FRANKLIN RICH WORE GARDENING GLOVES AND held a pair of shears in one hand and the cut end of the phone cord in the other.

I dropped my hand to my side, still holding the phone.

The last time I'd been face-to-face with the principal was at the school. He'd been understanding about Lily's life and apologetic about the lack of a coach for David. He'd chased after me and handed off David's backpack—the backpack filled with evidence that linked David to the crimes.

"You thought you could frame a seventeen-year-old boy for the murder of his father," I said. "You wanted us all to think David did this."

"After the way his father abandoned him? David should have wanted his father dead. That's the most challenging aspect of my job—today's youth lacks the proper motivation."

"But why kill Gil Banks and Ed Bishop?"

"After Banks had his crisis of conscience, I didn't have

much of a choice. He had no problem producing the drugs, but when he heard my plans for distribution, he got cold feet."

I was temporarily confused, until I remembered what Jimmy had told me: Principal Rich was on a witch hunt after catching kids dealing behind the school. My mind filled in the gaps with the images of children playing at recess, of classrooms of young targets spilling out into the hallways, and of this singular figure of authority who oversaw it all. My stomach turned. "The prep school," I said. "You were the one distributing drugs to your students."

"It's never too early to teach your kids habits they'll keep for the rest of their lives," he said, his face twisting into a grimace. Gone were the traces of attractiveness, the charm, and confidence that comes with a position of power, and in its place were hints of greed and desperation. It was a toxic combination that I'd seen before on other desperate criminals, and it wasn't until that moment that I realized all of the people we'd told about David and Amber were going to show up at the house next door, not the one in which I was now trapped.

"That's why you killed Gil and Ed?" I asked.

"I killed them because I didn't need them anymore. Ed thought he could outrun me. Once I had his research from his computer, he was expendable." His mouth contorted into a grimace. "Funny thing about researchers. They document *everything*."

"But you gave me that information when I came to the school."

"Not *that* information. I gave you Ed's field research. You didn't think I was going to hand over my recipe and make it easy for the police, did you?

"And Gil? What about him?"

"He tried to blackmail me. Said I had to cut him in fifty-fifty or he'd go to the feds. I promised him a one-way ticket out of the country and told him to lay low while things cooled off, and then I killed him in his research lab with a clipping from one of the poisonous plants he and Ed grew. Serendipity, don't you think? One murder leads to the other murder in an endless loop to keep the police chasing their tails while I go on my merry way."

"The dirt," I said unexpectedly. "It came from the backyard."

"Ah, no. It came from your friend Donna's backyard. I didn't know Gil hired a private security company until too late, so I needed to keep her in check too. Did you know the soil in Highland park is just different enough from the soil here to make it identifiable?" He appeared pleased with himself. "Education really is a wonderful thing."

Lights shone on the front windows. I felt, for a second, that the cavalry had arrived, but it hadn't; these cars weren't here for me. They pulled into Harry's driveway. I didn't know how to let them know what was taking me so long, and by the time they came to check on me, it might be too late.

"Get comfortable, Madison. You're not going anywhere." Franklin adjusted his gloves. "There's a fresh grave out back that has your name on it."

I couldn't allow my imagination to run with the possibilities of what that meant. My legs were shaking, and my heart was thumping in my chest. I was terrified, but I had to appear unflustered. "Do you actually believe you can kill me without anyone noticing?"

"I don't have to kill you," he said. "I imagine six feet of dirt will take care of that part for me."

My stomach turned. I could run, but could I outrun him?

I could scream, but would anyone hear me?

I could fight, but unarmed against a pair of gardening shears, would I come away unscathed?

Behind me, the front door opened. I turned and saw Jimmy enter. He looked straight at me and then pulled his AirPods out of his ears. "Hey, boss," he said. "You were taking a long time with my table saw, so I came to get it myself." He looked in the living room. "Where is it?"

I stood as still as I could, willing Jimmy to leave. He came into the kitchen and lifted the saw from the table. He was about to depart when he turned back. "Hey, Principal Rich," he said. "What are you doing here?"

Franklin stepped away from the shadows and put his hands behind his back to hide the gardening shears. I had a flash, a memory, of something Jimmy had said.

I locked eyes with my seventeen-year-old employee and hoped he trusted me enough to take direction, even if it went against what he'd been taught. "Jimmy, remember what you said you wanted to give your principal?" I asked.

"Yes, but—"

I forced a smile and nodded. "I think now is a once-in-a-lifetime opportunity."

Jimmy didn't waste any time. He dumped the table saw on the counter, took two steps past me, and punched Franklin Rich in the face.

Things happened quickly after that.

I kicked the gardening shears out of Franklin's reach. Jimmy and I wrestled him to the floor and tied him up with his rope. My cell phone fell out of Franklin's pocket when he hit the floor, and my first call was to Tex.

"I'm already on my way," he said.

"Tell your detectives to get here too," I said. "I've got Franklin Rich tied up in Lily's new kitchen room. He just confessed to the murders of Gil and Ed."

CHAPTER TWENTY-NINE

After Franklin Rich was arrested for the murders of two meth-cooking botanists, life became blissfully peaceful for a while. I never did get Jimmy to chop that wooden table in half for my windows, but I did fill the empty space with a variety of wicker picnic baskets containing family-sized bags of potato chips. Gabe said it was the best window display he'd ever seen. I would have liked Adam to second the notion, but he was busy looking for salamanders in my parking lot.

Too much had transpired with the house on Cinderella Lane for Lily to want to live there, so it was with a heavy amount of resistance that I directed her to a team of house flippers and asked them to make her an offer. One question realtors should start asking about properties: has a body ever been buried out back? To date, that information hasn't been included as part of disclosure.

Even our living spaces quieted down a bit. Lily and the

boys moved into Tex's townhouse, but Tex, having come out of the past week worse for wear, moved in with me. The next day, my fridge was filled with Lone Star Beer, and a second dog bowl joined Rocky's on a mat in the kitchen. I quietly changed the sheets to white trimmed with blue embroidery and tucked my pink floral ones into the hamper. There were times I actively chose to push Tex out of his comfort zone, but he'd had a difficult week, and this time, I took pity.

Two things about my business had become exceedingly clear: only one member of my two-person staff had a passion for mid-century modern design. And having seen Effie's pro/con list on my satellite office desk, I knew what I had to do.

So, within the span of twenty-four hours, Effie was let go from Mad for Mod with the first ever severance package. She accepted a position in Big Bro Security's IT department. Lily filled my vacancy. And Jimmy, dear, sweet, spontaneous, the-principal-is-out-to-get-me Jimmy, was offered the first-ever (and most likely last) Mad for Mod scholarship for design school upon his high school graduation. I met with the schoolboard to smooth out the damage done to his transcripts with the baseball brownie incident.

After the news broke about his involvement in taking down his meth-dealing principal, Jimmy's popularity soared. He asked out Trish McCardell and she made a batch of brownies just for him.

As for Amber Rich, she quietly transferred to another school. It was another domino fall in the grand game of moving on from tragedy, and I can't say I blamed her.

I lined up my calendar with three months of new jobs and

redecorated my guest bedroom in a baseball theme. I covered the wall behind the bed with colorful vintage pennants, and had Jimmy build a headboard out of old bats. I set a tall, clear vase atop the dresser and filled it with worn and dirty baseballs. Tex invited Adam to stay over for the weekend, but after he saw the room, I didn't think he was going to leave.

And me? I closed Mad for Mod for the week, and while Lily and her boys finally unloaded their truck of personal belongings, I sorted through the estate of my parents. I took time with each piece, running my hand over a walnut chifforobe that had belonged to my mother, and a davenport that we used to share on movie night, me wedged between her and my dad. I took an afternoon break and relaxed on one of two divans upholstered in celery green, with a round floral pillow tucked under my neck, and I stared at my showroom ceiling and then closed my eyes and let my long-suppressed memories wash over me. From the other side of the room, I heard four boys between the ages of ten and fifty-two. I heard two dogs barking. I heard the door open and a woman call out, "Grub's here! Get it while it's hot!"

And I realized I'd lost the family I knew thirty years ago, but when I wasn't looking, I'd gained a new one. Filled with family and friends, lovers and pets, colleagues, and employees and—God help me—homicide detectives. I sat up from the divan and watched as they crowded around the two Sues, who'd shown up with enough takeout bags to appease the whole lot of them.

While the others flocked to Ling and Sue to claim their lunches, an unexpected visitor walked in: Nasty. She held Huxley, who had his head nestled against her and his arms draped over her shoulders. She zeroed in on the crowd to the right, then looked away and found me on the divan. I sat up and smiled. She approached me. I scooted to the side and made room for her to sit down.

"Hi," I said. "I didn't expect to see you so soon."

"I wanted to thank you."

"Don't mention it. I already told you Effie's great. You're going to love her."

"This isn't about Effie." Huxley woke and fussed. Nasty kissed his head. "If I want something, I take it. I don't wait around for someone to offer it to me."

"It's your most attractive quality," I told her, not without a tinge of both sarcasm and envy.

"It's yours too," she said. "You may not realize this, Madison, but we're not all that different. When the police showed up at my house, I had one concern." She tipped her head toward Huxley. "This guy. There's a reason I asked you to watch out for him. I knew you wouldn't let me down."

I thought about Nasty being escorted to the police station. About promising to take care of Huxley. About taking Huxley with us to speed dating where he sat in the back of Connie's Miata while Connie and I swapped clothes in the parking lot. I thought about sending Huxley off with Connie while Lola and I went to the house on Cinderella Lane and discovered a body in the backyard, and about how Connie had repurposed Wojo's training cage into a playpen at Tex's house. I imagined Huxley behind those aluminum bars, staring out, and I wondered if I'd been responsible for permanent damage to his maturity cycle.

"He won't remember," she said.

"He won't remember what?" I asked, feigning ignorance.

"Whatever happened between me leaving the party and now. He knows about fifty words. He hasn't started stringing them together into sentences, and even if he could, I doubt he'd give me details about what happened."

I reached my hand out and cupped it around Huxley's. He turned his head and his face opened into a smile. He giggled and bounced on Nasty's knee, and then pointed his hand across the room where Tex stood with the boys.

An unpleasant scent filled the air. Huxley wriggled back and forth and called out, "Poopy poopy poop!"

Nasty leaned down and sniffed. "I'll be right back." She turned him back around and stood, cradling him to her body. "Thanks, Madison. For being someone I can rely on. You're starting to feel like another sister." She carried Huxley away and, seconds later, Tex took her place.

He handed me a waxy In-N-Out takeout bag. "Do you want to be alone?" he asked.

"Not particularly."

He lowered himself to the vacated divan cushion while I removed a burger from the take-out bag. He tore open my bag and helped himself to fries. "Crazy week," he said.

"Sure was."

"With the boys at my place and Lily working for you, I don't see things calming down any time soon."

"You're probably right."

"You okay with all this?"

I took in the sight in front of me: Gabe holding a French fry over Wojo's head, David laughing with George about something on his phone, Adam massaging oil into his new catcher's mitt. I saw Rocky nipping at Adam's ankles, and

Lily assisting Nasty with Huxley's diaper change, all within the four walls of my satellite studio.

"I'm okay with all this."

"Good," he said. He slung his arm around my shoulders and pulled me toward him, then kissed my temple. "Welcome to the family, Night."

ACKNOWLEDGMENTS

It's impossible for me to write a new Madison Night mystery without reflecting on where she started: as an emotionally closed off woman with a broken heart and a bum knee, determined to live a fulfilling life with her Shih Tzu puppy and her business. Eleven books in and the business and puppy are still there, but so is a social group she and I never imagined. This series may have stopped after three books if you hadn't embraced her as you have, and I am grateful that you did! A nod to Henery Press, for encouraging me to write book four, and for granting the rights to use the image of Rocky on the cover.

Thank you to Virgil and Lynn at Red Adept Editing, for both your effective edit and your patience while I requested more time. I appreciate your flexibility. Thank you also to Amy Ross Jolly, Melissa Fosseen, Janet Graham, Barbara Hackel, Shawna Gregg, and Katherine Munro for your eagle eyes and eleventh-hour feedback.

My eternal thank you goes out to members of the Polyester Posse. Thank you for helping to spread the word about Madison's latest mystery!

To members of the Weekly DiVa Club: your eagerness to dead people will never cease to entertain me! Special thank you to Barbara Hill, Kelley Hawks, and Virginia Healy for offering the use of your names as previous owners of Madison Night's wardrobe choices.

Thank you go my writing group, Gigi Pandian, Lisa Q. Matthews, and Ellen Byron, who are always up for a brainstorming session or a plot-point gut-check. I'm happy to have you in my corner.

A Madison Night Mystery would not exist without the body of work of Doris Day, and I continue to be inspired by her life and movies regularly.

And, lastly, my eternal thanks to my readers. I'm thrilled that you've embraced my books and hope to keep bringing you fun, fashionable fiction for years to come.

ABOUT THE AUTHOR

Four-time award nominee and national bestselling author Diane Vallere writes smart, funny, and fashionable character-based mysteries. After a career in luxury retailing, she traded fashion accessories for accessories to murder. Diane started her own detective agency at age ten and has maintained a passion for shoes, clues, and clothes ever since.

Get girl talk, book talk, and life talk when you join the Weekly Diva Club at dianevallere.com/weekly-diva.

ALSO BY

The Pajama Frame

Lover Come Hack

Apprehend Me No Flowers

Teacher's Threat

The Kill of It All

Love Me or Grieve Me

Please Don't Push Up the Daisies

Sylvia Stryker Outer Space Mysteries

Murder on a Moon Trek

Scandal on a Moon Trek

Hijacked on a Moon Trek

Framed on a Moon Trek

Material Witness Mysteries

Suede to Rest

Crushed Velvet

Silk Stalkings

Tulle Death Do Us Part

Costume Shop Mystery Series

A Disguise to Die For

Masking for Trouble

Dressed to Confess